Lily Dragon

Also by Mary Ellis

THE ARCTIC FOX

MARY ELLIS

ILLUSTRATED BY RACHAEL PHILLIPS

An imprint of HarperCollins*Publishers*

For Andy and Matilda with love

With thanks to Graham Hutt at the British Library

First published in Great Britain in hardback by Collins in 1999
This edition published in paperback in 2000
Collins is an imprint of HarperCollins*Publishers* Ltd
77-85 Fulham Palace Road, Hammersmith, London W6 8JB

The HarperCollins website address is:
www.fireandwater.com

3 5 7 9 8 6 4

ISBN 0 00 675458 9

Printed and bound in Great Britain by
Omnia Books Limited, Glasgow

CHAPTER ONE
The Farm

MY MOTHER SAID that all this happened because I was born in the Year of the Dragon. I had an impulsive streak that she warned me about many times. She said it would lead me into heaps of trouble.

I'll always remember the evening when it began. I'd sat for hours in the oak tree at the end of the clover field and watched darkness settle over the river. I sat until the barns and trees became shadowy silhouettes and a light came on in a distant farmhouse. I think I had deliberately ignored signs that our farm was in trouble: Mum had got a job at the University, the farm shop was closing and Dad was looking strained and tired.

I was born on the farm. It was the only life I had ever known. My brother Tom and I loved running across the fields every morning on our way to school. In the evenings we'd stop in the woods, building caverns and grottoes until it was time for tea. These places were a part of me, as constant as a heartbeat. Or so I thought.

As I crossed the cobbles to the house I glanced through the kitchen window. Mum was sitting at the kitchen table, her head in her hands. I saw my father kiss her gently on the head and leave the room. He was stooped and walking in that sad way that was now familiar to me. I opened the door.

There was an uncharacteristic stillness about the house. My mother looked up, her eyes full of tears.

Suddenly I felt very scared. I had never seen her cry.

"Lily Dragon, come here," she said, "and sit by me. I can't keep this from you any longer. I know how much the farm means to you. For your Dad and me it has held so much joy. It was a new start for me, away from the turmoil of China. We've tried everything to avoid this."

"But what?" I cried out in desperation.

"We are losing the farm. The shop didn't work out and we owe too much money to the bank. It's hard for farmers to make money these days. Even the weather has been against us for the last two years. I'm so sorry, Lily."

I felt very cold. I was shaking. My mother got a rug off the sofa and wrapped it around me, hugging me close to her.

"What will happen?" I whispered.

"A farm consortium want to buy it from us."

"But they'll destroy it," I cried. "They'll take away the bluebell woods and cut down the hedges to make huge fields. Then what will the rabbits and birds do?... And chemicals Mum, they'll use pesticides and ruin everything you and Dad worked for. What will happen to the cows and calves? It's lambing time soon... And the chickens... they won't be able to live a free life any more. There must be something we can do."

My mother clasped both my hands and spoke to me with a strange, firm tone.

"There's something I want you to do Lily Dragon, and you've got to be very brave and fearless. I've thought about it very hard. It's about our trip to China. I know we've planned it for so long, but Lily – your Dad and I cannot possibly go now. You must go for us and take Tom. Your brother is too young to know all this. You know how I've always longed for you to meet Aunt Li and your Grandma Tsui. We cannot disappoint them after all these weeks of planning. It would mean Tom needn't know about the farm until it is settled and your Dad and I have found a new house for us all."

She held on to me tightly as I sat unable to speak.

Chapter Two
Grandpa Zhang

We were to leave for China in a week's time. We had planned this trip for months – in fact Mum had been waiting for years for China to be safe enough to return to. We had even been given time off school so that the trip could take place over the Chinese New Year. It was to be the lucky Year of the Tiger. I had been counting the days until our departure. Being half Chinese, I'd always longed to go there and to visit Mum's family, but now I moved like a sleepwalker. I was searching for an answer to losing the farm.

The following evening Tom got back from staying with a friend. My brother was born in the Year of the Monkey, and it couldn't be a better way of summing him up. His silly face and wild ideas made me laugh. We were three years apart but we'd always played together.

"Race you to the barn Lil," he said, putting on his rollerblades. "Come on, I've got the torch. First one there gets to name the new calf."

But I didn't have the heart. I felt helpless and he was completely carefree.

"Not now Tom. I've got to think."

"Oh well," he shrugged. "Then I'll call it Biff," and he rushed off singing down to the barn.

How could I name another animal knowing that I'd never see it grow up?

After supper, while Dad was over with the new calf, Mum sat Tom down and told him about the trip to China.

"Lil, have you heard?" Tom cried. "It's just us going to China now. Mum and Dad can't leave the farm."

"Yes," said my mother quickly. "I told Lily yesterday."

I started clearing the plates. I had to hide my tears. I didn't want to let Mum down, but I didn't know how to be enthusiastic about going to China and leaving the farm. I knew I might never see it again.

When I went back into the room, Tom said:

"Lil, we'll go all that way on our own! Just wait till I tell everyone. We'll see pandas. George says there are only a thousand left in the world. Aunt Li will meet us off the plane in Beijing and then she'll take us to Grandma Tsui for the New Year. Just imagine Lil, at last we'll see a real Chinese New Year!" He paused to draw breath. "Mum, tell us the story of Grandpa Zhang and the treasure box."

"Well, I will," smiled my mother, "if Lily comes and sits next to us. Just as Aunt Li and I used to sit with your grandmother to hear the same story.

"Over three hundred years ago your Grandpa Zhang was a court artist in the palace of the forbidden city during the Qing Dynasty. He was very gifted, but he also had a reputation for making the other artists and courtiers laugh. Some disapproved of him, but there was one wise old man who always kept a watchful eye over him.

"One day the wise old man came to Grandpa Zhang for help.

"'The Emperor Ch'ien-Lung is living in too grand a way,' he said. 'He is not thinking of his people or of the Western countries who want to take our land. Rebellion and invasion are too close to ignore. I am afraid that there will be a war, and that will mean the destruction of the Emperor's art treasures. We must take some of the most precious items and travel to a land beyond the touch of war. We will hide them until peace comes. Only then will we tell the Emperor how we have looked after China's treasures.'

"So one night the two of them loaded the treasures on to a wagon and went on a journey that took many weeks. They travelled far across Chinese territory to a place of safety. Once there, they recruited workmen loyal to the Emperor. These men helped them hide the treasure – but they were blindfolded so they never knew the way to the hiding place.

"On the journey home the wise man, who had been made frail by their journey, became ill and grew increasingly sick. Just before he died he held on to Grandpa Zhang and said:

"'The secret is in your hands. Only reveal it to our rulers when we are assured of peace and hope in China again.'

"Grandpa Zhang was young. He watched as wars came and went, but there was never peace. Once he had retired, he would take his children and grandchildren to his workshop and show them a tiny treasure box that he had carved out of wood.

"'In this,' he would explain, 'are thirty miniature replicas of the treasures I hid for China.'"

"What are replicas?" interrupted Tom.

"Copies," said Mum, "miniature copies. When the family would question Grandpa Zhang further, he would simply sit back in his chair and close his eyes with a mysterious smile on his face. Peace never did come to China in Grandpa Zhang's lifetime, so the secret of the treasure box died with him."

"Did you ever see it Mum, the treasure box?" I suddenly asked.

"Yes, I remember once when I was little my

grandmother showed it to Aunt Li and me. It was most beautiful, with a green jade dragon disc set in the top. I think it was locked and I remember Grandma saying that she hadn't been able to open it."

"I hope we see it when we're there," said Tom happily.

"Yes... we must," I agreed quietly, as an idea began to dawn on me.

Before going to bed, Mum always lit a candle and sat by the fire to read. She said it reminded her of her childhood and put life in perspective. I tiptoed over to her once Tom was in bed.

"Oh Lily sweetheart, it's you," she said. "I've been meaning to say that I haven't told Grandma and Li Li the real reason for our not coming to China. I'll explain it all to them when we know more. I don't want them to worry and they're longing to see you both."

"It's all right Mum, it's settled. I'll go to China with Tom *and* I'll save the farm for you. I know what to do now."

My mother smiled sadly and ruffled my hair, not understanding.

"I'm going to find the treasure," I explained. "Grandpa Zhang meant one of us to. I know it. The time has come."

"Well, I suppose China's future is more peaceful and hopeful than ever before," said Mum, smiling. "That's a very sweet idea Lily, thank you. But remember it all happened three hundred years ago."

I knew she wasn't taking me seriously. She had

too much on her mind. It didn't matter. I hugged her. I went back to my room and took my suitcase off the top of the wardrobe there and then. Once a dragon has an idea she must follow it through to its conclusion, no matter what may happen. I'd start with the treasure box. That's what I would do.

CHAPTER THREE

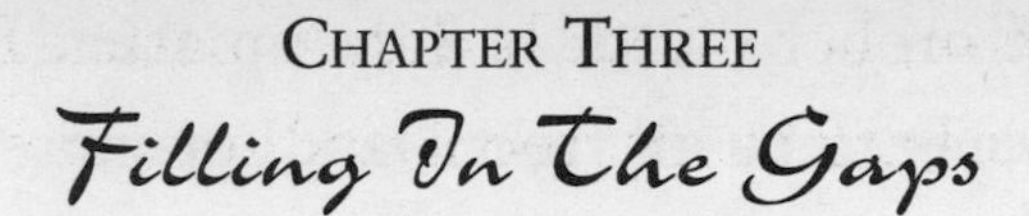

Filling In The Gaps

NEVER LOOK BACK *at the setting sun, only forward to the rising moon.* The words rushed through my head as we packed the car and then drove through the golden hedgerows to say goodbye to Dad. He was working on the fence at the end of the meadow. A perfect winter sun was setting and our plane was leaving at eight o'clock that evening.

Dad rushed over to say goodbye, laughing and joking with Tom.

"What took you so long? You haven't got your rollerblades in there, have you Tom?"

"Yes, but it's the books for Aunt Li that take up most room," grumbled Tom.

Just as I was getting back into the car Dad grabbed my hand and hugged me once more.

"I'm sorry about the farm, Lily," he whispered.

"Maybe there'll be another time up ahead."

"It's going to be all right Dad, I promise."

I'd been fighting a lump in my throat, but as we drove away and I watched Dad standing on the tractor waving us out of sight, tears rolled down my cheeks.

"Cheer up Lil," said Tom. "We'll be back in a month. It'll all still be here, the farm won't blow away."

But by the time we said goodbye to Mum at the airport, I was the brave one.

"I wish you and Dad were coming too," Tom said suddenly as he hugged Mum outside the departure gate.

"I do too my sweethearts, with all my heart. Give Grandma and Li Li a big hug from me." Mum blinked back her tears. "Now don't forget my messages and the letters for everyone. Enjoy yourselves and be careful, Tom and Lily Dragon – look after each other. Remember to send me lots of postcards!"

For the first time in ages Tom walked next to me, grabbing on to the back of my cardigan. Once we were on the plane though, he was back to his old self. He gave me detailed accounts of all the safety instructions and exit doors – "Just in case," he added, "because we are 'unaccompanied minors', whatever that means." He felt even more special when he had an invitation from the captain to go up to the cockpit.

Tom ate everything on his dinner tray and most of what was on mine. I wasn't hungry anyway. Afterwards he fell fast asleep with his earphones on and a smile on his face. Now I had a chance to think.

One of Mum's messages to Aunt Li and my

grandmother was to apologise for never coming home herself. You see, my mother's life story was complicated. She left China at fourteen. That was in 1965, when revolution had stirred a "madness" (as my mother called it) in the country. Schools and learning were seen as dangerous and bad. Great bonfires were made of books. Children were being sent away from their families and schools, to work in the fields. Gentleness was seen as weakness, and even a girl's long hair was frowned on. My mother's two long plaits had to be cut off.

My mother was a very clever, gentle little girl. Even her name 'Bin Bin' meant softness. My grandmother was very worried about my mother's future. She knew it was only a matter of time before she'd be sent away. My grandmother had a friend who worked for the railways, and he agreed to smuggle my mother on to a train leaving for Hong Kong. Once there, she'd be looked after by relatives and she'd be able to go to school. So Mum arrived in Hong Kong, hidden under the bench seat of a train. She was too afraid to come out until my grandmother's relatives came on to the train to find her. She stayed with them and even went to University there.

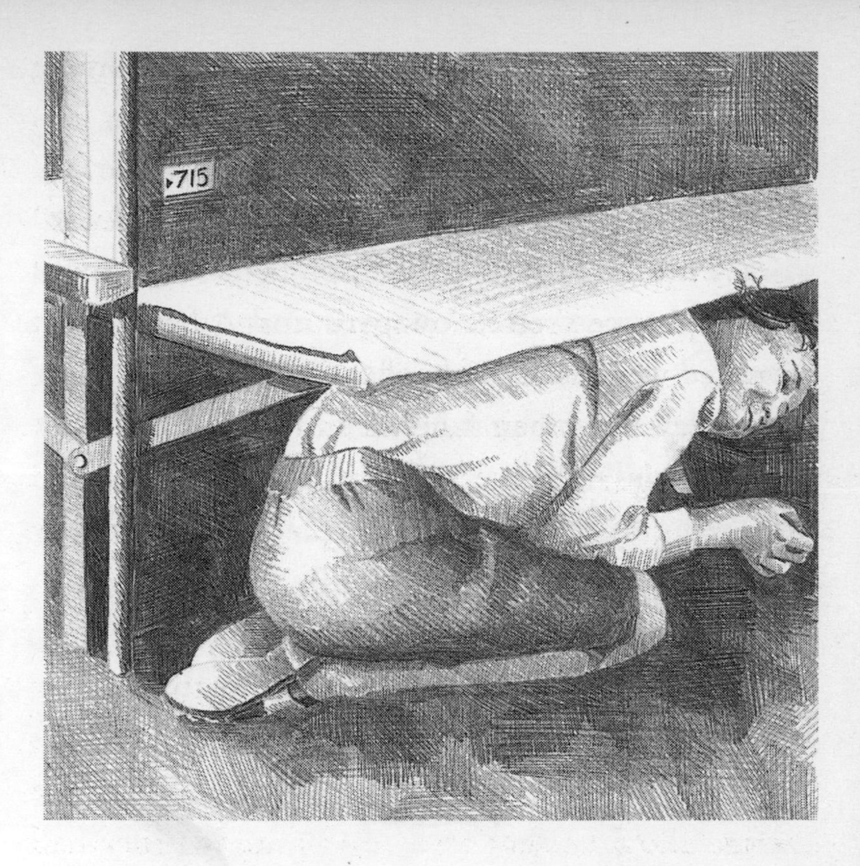

It was when Mum was going to one of her classes that she happened to sit next to my dad on a bus. They started talking. He was on his way through Hong Kong to Australia to learn about sheep farming. Dad gave up his sightseeing to sit on the University steps for days, waiting to see Mum on her way home. They rode together on the bus, and fell in love on the way back to Mum's house!

Mum said she always felt guilty because Aunt Li, her elder sister, hadn't been so fortunate in her education. She had been taken away from University and her studies in medicine, in order to work with the buffalo in the rice fields. Although these bad times were now over and Aunt Li had managed to qualify as a doctor in Beijing, my mother felt terrible that her sister had lost all those years of studying. For my part, I always thought that being able to stay outside all day sounded more fun than going to school. But Mum said that's because I was lucky. I would never know how terrible life is when the freedom to learn is taken away.

I must have fallen asleep, because I woke up when the stewardess patted me gently and held out a hot towel for me to wipe my face. We had landed for refuelling. Once we took off again Tom and I both fell back to sleep, our necks aching from being squashed in our seats for so long.

The plane descended to Hong Kong's airport on Lantau Island. This time we had to get out and take the 'Dragon Airways' flight to Beijing in

China. We couldn't help feeling a bit disappointed when we realised that it was just an ordinary plane. So while Tom played with a computer game that he'd bought at the airport, I imagined we were riding a true Chinese dragon with a fiery purple and red mane, all the way to Aunt Li in China.

CHAPTER FOUR
Aunt Li

TOM HELD ON to the strap of my bag as we walked, rather dazed, into an Arrivals hall full of people. A sea of faces looked at us enquiringly, but one woman, only a little taller than me, rushed forwards. Her dark hair was pulled back into a bun, her face looked very strict – and for a moment Tom and I wondered if we'd done something wrong. We both hesitated, when suddenly she smiled and her whole face lit up. She grabbed my hands in hers and kissed them over and over again.

"*Nihao* Lily, and this is Tom. You are both welcome, so welcome!"

"Aunt Li?" said Tom questioningly.

"But of course, yes! I am your Aunt Li and you are so like my Bin Bin. She sent me photos. This is a great moment. But we must rush, the *gongongqiche* will be going without us."

"She means the bus," I whispered to Tom. I only knew a little Chinese.

Picking up both our heavy bags Aunt Li set off at a furious pace across the airport hall. We had to run to keep up with her. She went out into a great crowd of people who were all waiting for the doors of a bus to open.

"Stay close," she ordered. She shouted "Go!" as the doors opened, and without a backwards look she shoved her way past the other people on to the bus, clearing a path for us. No one looked surprised or angry at her behaviour. When she'd sat us both down on a seat, she straightened her jacket and patted her hair.

"There," she exclaimed. "We're off."

"That was great, Aunt Li," said Tom with open admiration.

"I've never ever seen so many people on a bus before," I said, thinking aloud.

"Wait until you see the train station," said Aunt Li, looking rather proud.

What was amazing was the way everyone on the bus remained calm and dignified despite the overcrowding. They only looked surprised when the bus went over a bump and they accidentally fell against each other.

Aunt Li winked at us. After five or six stops she said: "We're here, move quickly!"

Before we had a chance to think, we were picked up and lowered carefully out of the bus window and down into a crowd.

"Here, this is Dow, my second cousin," she said as she beckoned over an elderly man. "He's got the cart. I'll go with him and the bags. You'll go in the pedicab."

Dow got on his bicycle and pulled Aunt Li, who was perched on top of our bags like a crow, in a cart behind him. Meanwhile we sat in the pedicab. This was a special cart with a covered roof drawn by a very gruff man on a bike. He kept muttering and spitting on to the road as he pulled us through the twinkling and unfamiliar world of Beijing.

Mum had warned us that it would be bitterly cold at night, and it was. Tom's teeth started to chatter, which made us both laugh. Once we had started we couldn't stop. I think it was relief and our amazement at all the strange things that we kept seeing around us.

The streets started to grow narrower as we left the modern roads behind. We continued our journey through winding alleyways. People were sitting outside their houses playing cards, talking and reading by lamplight. The roar of traffic was replaced by music from within the passing houses and the sound of the cart bumping over cobblestones.

"We're home," cried Aunt Li at last. She cleared her throat as if she was going to make a speech. Dow sat down on our bags. The pedicab driver spat once more and cycled off, still muttering to himself.

"Welcome to the Old City," she continued. "Our family home since Grandpa Zhang worked at the palace. Of course we now share it with five other families, but that is justice and life. We are so proud to bring Bin Bin's children into this place."

"We're very glad to be here," I said, speaking for Tom too. "We've been longing to meet you, Aunt Li."

Aunt Li seized my hands again and put them to her forehead. After wiping her eyes with a huge white handkerchief, she carried the two bags through the gates. Dow waved goodbye to us and set off in his cart once again.

We stepped into an inner courtyard. Tiled and curved roofs, like those we'd only seen in folk tales, hung over a porch that was supported by arches. It ran in a quadrangle around us. Bird cages, onions and baskets hung from the eaves. Two people who were playing ping pong in the courtyard stopped to stare at us. Aunt Li made the thumbs-up sign to them. Then she led us past a small stone dragon, through a swing door and into the room that was her home.

We didn't get a chance to look around because Aunt Li immediately sat us down at a little table and lit a burner underneath a pot of water placed in the centre of the table. From out of a tiny tiled corner of the room she brought plate after plate of chicken, fish, chinese leaf and bowls of soy and sesame sauce. Delighted by our surprised faces, she laughed.

"Yes, yes, you see now that the water is boiling so you cook your own food. Then you dip it into the sauces, and then you eat it! *Huoguo*, it is called – Mongolian Hot Pot. I'll start!"

And she did, with great gusto. It was delicious, and once again there was silence as we ate, trying to use our chopsticks. We'd been practising at home for a few days before our trip.

"And now," said Aunt Li, "Dragon Well Tea to drink in honour of Lily Dragon!"

When we had finished, Tom suddenly looked very sleepy. Aunt Li led him to a large cosy bed and he was soon fast asleep. I think he had worn himself out trying to pick up the food that kept dropping off his chopsticks and splashing in the sauce. Aunt Li thought this was very funny and she giggled every time he did it.

I was feeling really tired, so Aunt Li said it was bedtime for all of us. I realised that I was to sleep in the same bed as Tom. There wasn't another – Aunt Li had given us hers. She kissed me goodnight, went over to a sleeping bag and climbed in. Soon she started to snore.

I gazed at the huge wooden beams above me. I remembered Dad chopping wood to make us a treehouse in the bluebell woods, and Mum laughing and telling us how the Chinese believe that chopped wood is still alive, and to live in a wooden house is terribly lucky. The farm and our life there seemed very far away now. I was glad that Tom was close by. I reminded myself to ask Aunt Li about Grandpa Zhang's treasure box in the morning. The last thing I remember thinking was a hope that if these wooden beams were still alive, they might be watching over us in this strange country of our ancestors.

Chapter Five

Kites and Crickets

Something small and hard landed quite suddenly on the bed and woke me with a start. I couldn't think where I was for a moment. I sat up and found a peanut on my sheet.

"*Duibuqi*," said a quiet voice.

I turned around to see a boy and a girl, sitting close together on Aunt Li's sofa.

The girl's face was very solemn and serious. "Sorry," she repeated, and pointed at the boy. He grinned and threw another peanut. This time, I ate it. The girl stood up, clutching a piece of paper. She came over and handed it to me.

Bin Bin's children, I've gone to work at the hospital. Xing Xi and Xing Ou (twins) who live next door are going to stay with you. Their New Year holiday has started so I have asked them to show you our city. We'll leave on the train tonight for Chengdu. Blessings, Aunt Li.

"*Nihao*, hello," I said, then "Lily," pointing to myself.

"Xing Ou," said the girl. She pointed at the boy. "Xing Xi."

The boy offered me another peanut in its shell. This time I took the shell and threw it on to Tom, who was still fast asleep. The twins laughed. Then we all had a go. It took a lot of shells to wake Tom. At last he sat up with a startled face. After I'd explained about Aunt Li's letter, he scrambled off the bed and shook the twins' hands in a rather awkward manner. By way of further introduction he showed them his rollerblades. Then, still in his pyjamas and a jumper, he helped Xing Ou to rollerblade round and round the bamboo garden in the middle of the quadrangle.

After we had all had a go, we sat on the porch steps by the stone dragon and ate the breakfast that Aunt Li had left for us. There was rice porridge, fried peanuts, and pork in such a hot sauce that tears ran down our faces. Xing Ou ran to get us some tea. We were friends now and words had not been needed.

We were a funny group when we finally set off. Xing Ou and Xing Xi had been asked to look after their baby cousin "Little Swan", and the mother had carefully strapped Little Swan to Xing Ou's back. Little Swan held on tightly as we stepped out into the teeming street market that surrounded Aunt Li's house. We walked among fruit sellers, drink stalls and the delicious smell of pancakes cooking.

The twins seemed to know everyone in these narrow lanes. People waved and greeted us, occasionally patting Little Swan and touching my brown hair. My mother had told me that this might happen.

Xing Ou and Xing Xi took us to an old building like a tower, not very far away. We climbed to the top, and from there we had a bird's eye view over the city. We could see the gilded, sloping roofs of the Forbidden City, where Chinese Emperors had lived and ruled for hundreds of years. Fantastic kites tossed wildly in the cold wind above a nearby park.

"New Year," said Xing Ou in English, pointing at the kites and laughing self-consciously.

"Kite flying for New Year," I said quietly. "We did it once with Mum on the hill above the dairy."

The noise of the wind on the tower startled Little Swan and she began to cry. We ran to the park and sat on the grass eating pancakes and noodles that the twins had bought from a little cart.

Little Swan crawled over our legs and played wheelbarrows with Tom and me. Then we all lay in the grass watching the kites fly above us. The most beautiful kite of all had a dragon's head and a caterpillar's body. It danced on the wind like a magical sea serpent. Xing Ou asked the man flying it if I could have a go. My hands trembled as the force of the wind tugged at the strings. Just as I felt my feet leaving the ground everyone ran to grasp the kite strings. We fell together in a big heap. Little Swan was screaming with excitement now. The kite man wheezed and scolded us in Chinese.

It was then that Xing Xi and Xing Ou led us to the bird market. Many, many people were bustling along little alleyways of booths full of cages and extraordinary coloured birds. The twins stopped by a booth that was lit up like a magic lantern. A harmonious song came in waves from within. The booth was stocked to the rafters with miniature wooden cages and boxes. An old man was sitting warming himself by a heater.

"But they must be tiny birds," I exclaimed.

"*Xishuai, xishuai*," said Xing Xi earnestly. We didn't understand. The old man took down a box and opened it. He took out an insect. It was a dark-looking grasshopper.

"A CRICKET!" said Tom. "It's them singing!"

Little Swan had started to imitate their song, which made us laugh.

Tom delved deep into his trouser pockets. "Lily, I'm going to get one, and then I'll set him free when we go to the countryside. Aunt Li promised we'd go to the countryside. He'll be happier in the wild."

Dusty and exhausted, we arrived back at Aunt Li's home. Tom was clutching a little box with holes in the top. The cricket, named "Lucky Peanut" by Tom, was lovingly shown to Aunt Li when she returned from work.

"Well done Bin Bin's children, a good choice of companion. He'll need some cabbage, a good street vendor's cabbage. I saw some left in the street just outside the gates."

Tom and the twins ran off to get it. Aunt Li was straightening her room, collecting her clothes and belongings into a bag. We were leaving to visit Great Grandma Tsui in Chengdu in half an hour's time. I wondered if everything was always done in a rush in China. I hadn't even had a chance to ask Aunt Li about Grandpa Zhang's treasure box.

"Aunt Li, do you remember the story of the treasure box made by Grandpa Zhang? Mother said Great Grandma Tsui showed it to you both when you were little."

Aunt Li stopped bustling and stood quite still for a minute. Once again her solemn face made me wonder if she was going to be cross with me. She went over to a set of drawers and took out an old tin box.

"Bin Bin's Lily, that is a great thing to remind me of... and it is a strange coincidence. Good fortune for the New Year. You see, the family next door live in Grandpa Zhang's old workshop room. They found this in a little opening in the wall. I'd forgotten… I've been meaning to ask Grandma Tsui about it for a long time now." She took out a tiny rectangular piece of metal with two grooves on one side and one on the other. "It's a key to an old Chinese lock."

"You mean that it could open the treasure box?" I said with excitement.

"Yes, that's what I remember… a Chinese lock. There's a chance. We'll take it with us to Chengdu and ask Grandma Tsui."

Chapter Six
The Train

ONCE AGAIN WE were following Aunt Li as she hurried through crowds of people, this time under the high vaulted ceiling of the station hall. Her yellow coat was like the Pied Piper's cloak. We walked in single file through a sea of people milling around us. Xing Xi and Xing Ou had come to see us off.

"Quick Xing Ou, look!" said Tom, pointing out a tiny kitten curled up in a basket. "And the chickens Lil, over there in the hampers."

"Four minutes," called Aunt Li as she pushed her way down on to the thronging platform.

At that moment a huge, black, gleaming train pulled into the station.

"A *steam* train!" I gasped.

The crowd surged forward as the train stopped.

People began climbing through open doors before the train had even come to a halt. A few ladies in uniform tried to keep order, pushing the crowds back with bamboo poles. Aunt Li grabbed Tom and me by the arm just as we were saying goodbye to the twins. She pushed us on to the train, passed us up the bags and then climbed on herself.

"Well done Bin Bin's children, this is a New Year crowd. Nothing like it on earth. Where is Lucky Peanut, Tom?"

"In my rucksack..." he gasped. "Oh – I forgot the cabbage, Lucky Peanut's cabbage! Look, Xing Ou's still holding it. I'll just get it."

Before we could stop him, Tom had jumped off the train and run to the twins. He got the cabbage just as the train started to pull away. Aunt Li and I watched in horror as Tom ran towards our outstretched hands and a fierce attendant pulled him back.

Aunt Li held on to me as I leaned as far as I could out of the door. I saw Xing Xi and Xing Ou running with Tom to the next carriage. Just as we turned a corner and the rest of the train disappeared from sight, I saw Tom holding on to one of the carriage doors.

"He's on Aunt Li, he's on," I shouted. Tears of relief were streaming down my face.

"Gracious heavens," said Aunt Li, handing me her white hankie, her face red with shock. "Just like Bin Bin," she said shaking her head.

"It's because he's a monkey," I said happily.

"Quick, we must go and find him," said Aunt Li.

We edged our way slowly down the train. Each carriage was crammed with passengers who had already made themselves comfortable for the long journey to come. They were playing cards, brewing tea. I even passed a fisherman who was selling crabs to some soldiers, but as we got to the end of the second carriage we realised there was no sign of Tom.

"Further," said Aunt Li hurriedly. "Keep going. It might have been the next carriage."

Luggage racks bulged with boxes. Children's laughter made a hollow echo around us. A panic was growing in the pit of my stomach. There was no sign of Tom anywhere.

Some people were unpacking a huge box of cabbages in the dining cart. "See," I cried, "there was more than enough food for one small cricket.

Why was he so silly to get off the train?"

Aunt Li sat down on her bag in a space in the corridor. "Lily," she said. Her voice was very calm. "If he didn't get on the train, the twins will call Grandma Tsui. They'll put him on the next train... I am certain."

"But Aunt Li," I said stubbornly, "I saw him holding on to the carriage door. He must be here." I couldn't even voice my other fear that he had fallen under the train as we came out of the station... down on to the tracks.

"Bin Bin's Lily, we'll go back again. We'll search each carriage."

My heart leapt several times when I saw the back of a boy's dark head. Each time it was a false alarm. There was no Tom in sight. Since we hadn't got round to claiming our reserved bunks, they had been quickly filled by several families.

Aunt Li's fighting spirit had left her. "Leave them," she said. "We'll go back through the train once more."

In return for our bunks, the families agreed to watch our luggage. The scent of tea and spices filled the air, Chinese pop music was piped over the carriage intercom, and the New Year festivities had begun without us. *But there was no Tom.*

Very quietly and firmly Aunt Li said, "We must talk to a guard. There might have been an accident."

The guards' carriage was the last one on the train. We stood outside the door. In the midst of the noise of engines and the sound of the train speeding over the tracks, a familiar chirping sound came from within the guards' carriage.

"Aunt Li, that sound," I said with excitement, "I know it... It's the sound of the..."

"CRICKET!" cried Aunt Li eagerly.

We banged on the guards' door. There was no answer, just more chirping and a guffaw of laughter. Seconds passed. We banged again. Finally the door was opened by a middle-aged man in guard's uniform. His sunken, skinny jaw was lit up with laughter and there, behind him and crouched next to a heater, was Tom. He was holding Lucky Peanut, who was singing happily.

"Lil, Aunt Li, you're here at last!" Tom exclaimed in a matter-of-fact way. "This is my friend Din Yuan. He pulled me on to the train."

The rest of our thirty-six-hour journey flew by in a mood of happiness and relief now that Tom was safe. The guard insisted that we stayed with him for both nights. We were relatives of his new-found friend. He had the dining car bring us *haougyou jiding*, which is chicken in oyster sauce. He was horrified that we had been in China for two days and hadn't yet tasted it.

When Tom and I started to yawn he tucked us into his bunk. Then he and Aunt Li talked late into the night, like old friends. While Lucky Peanut still sang in our dreams.

CHAPTER SEVEN
Grandma Tsui

WHEN WE ARRIVED in Chengdu, we discovered a city just as frantic and bustling as Beijing. The rickshaw came to a halt outside a plain concrete house, its roof sloping and ornate like an exotic hat.

"Grandma Tsui will be watching for us," said Aunt Li, pointing to the faces that peeped down at us from the windows above.

The door opened and out stepped an elderly woman with sparkling eyes and wispy white hair. She was small and bent. Startled by the daylight, she faltered a little and Aunt Li held her arm. She stood quite still and gazed at Tom and me. Aunt Li wiped her eyes. Grandma Tsui clasped our hands in hers. I knew then where my mother's smile came from.

After a moment she spoke, and Aunt Li translated:

"Grandma Tsui gives thanks that she has at last seen Bin Bin's precious children."

Still holding our hands, Grandma Tsui took us into her home. It seemed as busy as the station had been; full of noise, good spirits and people who nodded encouragingly at Tom and me.

The rooms were bursting with colour. Beautiful bright pieces of material were thrown over chairs and benches and the ceiling was hung with red and gold paper lanterns.

"Everyone is overjoyed that Bin Bin's children have arrived. There is good fortune this New Year because our family is together again," explained Aunt Li, becoming suddenly formal once again.

While Tom showed Grandma Tsui Lucky Peanut, Aunt Li told everyone the story of Tom and the train guard.

"And now it is time to make the Jaozi dumplings. Sit here at this table. Here's the dough and the mince."

"Mum makes these with us, Grandma, every New Year's Eve," I said, proud to show we knew the old traditions.

"It'll be a chance to remember the events of the

old year and to tell Grandma Tsui of your life, Lily."

Aunt Li translated Grandma Tsui's words. Grandma smiled and winked at us.

The dumplings were cooked in a huge pot of boiling water. Steam billowed from the low ceiling. A warm feeling of home enveloped us. Tom ate the dumplings as fast as we made them.

"If you eat all of them, soon your tummy will start to hurt," said Grandma Tsui, scolding him.

Meanwhile I spoke until my throat was dry

about our life growing up on the farm. But then, as that familiar ache at the loss of our home grew unbearable, I paused.

"Grandma Tsui, do you remember Grandpa Zhang's treasure box? I am so anxious to see it."

Grandma Tsui smiled, looked at the clock and stood up. She went over to Aunt Li, spoke quickly to her and then called us both over. Holding on to us for support, she walked out into the street to call for two bicycle rickshaws.

"Maybe she didn't hear your question?" whispered Tom as he obediently climbed into a rickshaw.

"Hush," said Aunt Li sternly. "She heard. Wait and see."

It was dusk, and we could hear drummers. We passed by a writhing dragon dancing to the rhythm of their music.

"The dragon parade," exclaimed Aunt Li. "Quick, we must hurry to the teahouse before the fireworks begin."

"Fantastic!" shouted Tom. "Lil, fireworks!"

Grandma Tsui patted my hand. "*Xiaode long*," she said. Which I knew meant "little dragon".

The teahouse was situated right by the river. The wind from the river scattered the scent of jasmine tea. We were perched on old bamboo chairs and given nuts to eat while we watched a couple play chess. Paper lanterns glowed brighter as darkness fell.

Suddenly, Grandma Tsui turned to us, and looking steadily into my eyes, spoke through Aunt Li.

"Lily, when the fireworks start, the owners of the teahouse will come out of the kitchen to watch. I want you to creep into the kitchen, go to the left-hand corner, and there you'll find a square floorboard by the oven's one clawed foot. If you press it, it will open and you will find a shoe box. Bring it to me quickly."

"I'll help," said Tom eagerly.

"No," said Grandma sharply, "you will stay with me. Watch the fireworks and enjoy yourself. One is safer than two for this purpose. This is Lily's destiny."

Chapter Eight

The Shoe Box

AT EIGHT O'CLOCK the fireworks started on the far side of the river. "Lily's destiny", Grandma Tsui had said. Was my destiny to be found in a shoe box? I wasn't scared, just excited. I knew I had to do what Grandma asked.

I moved outside the glow of the lanterns and into the darkness. I could watch the teahouse without anyone seeing me. When the owners came out of the teahouse kitchen and joined everyone near the river bank, I ran over to the door and slipped inside.

My heart was beating so loudly I could hear it above the cracking of the fireworks. The kitchen was deserted. Only a couple of ovens and tables full of old teapots and cups of tea. I crept over to the left-hand corner and knelt down by the oven's clawed foot. There was a mat in the way. I lifted it up and found the floorboard just as Grandma had said. I pressed on it and it opened with a loud creak. The dust from inside tickled my nose.

I could see the shoe box, but just as I reached in to get it, I heard footsteps. I saw two feet coming towards my corner. I froze and held my breath. Then a voice called out, and the footsteps retreated. I knew the voice was Aunt Li's. She had distracted them just before they caught me. This gave me a chance to grab the shoe box and scramble out of the back door. Tom must have guessed I couldn't get out the way I went in, and was there to meet me.

Tom and I ran back to Grandma Tsui. She took the shoe box and quickly put it in her bag. Together we watched the rest of the fireworks, but I can't really remember them now, just the lights, the bangs and the crowds... and the anticipation of seeing inside the box.

A man who had been playing chess at the next table knew Aunt Li. He insisted on giving us a lift home in his cart. Huddled together with us, Grandma told her story. Aunt Li translated, sometimes faltering to think of a word.

"At the start of the Cultural Revolution, when Bin Bin left for Hong Kong, I was worried that Grandpa Zhang's treasure box would be seen by some as a luxury. I was afraid it would be taken from us and destroyed. Your Aunt Li's best friend used to run the teahouse. She hid it in the shoe box under the floorboards for me. Then, during the Cultural Revolution, the teahouse was closed and abandoned.

"It is no accident that you ask about the treasure box now that the teahouse has just reopened. It is all part of a pattern."

"... and Aunt Li's found a key to a Chinese lock too," said Tom. "That's part of the pattern as well."

Grandma just nodded and smiled. "Indeed, you must take the treasure box, Lily. There's a dragon on the top of it. You are our dragon. Take it and use it wisely. There are patterns in life that cannot be dismissed. To do so would affect our destiny."

"I will use it wisely," I promised.

Back at the house Aunt Li showed us our room. There was just enough space for two bunks arranged like shelves. Aunt Li gave me the little metal key before she and Grandma Tsui said goodnight.

"If the key doesn't work, there's a metal file we can use to cut the lock off," added Aunt Li.

Tom and I crouched on the floor by the shoe box.

"Go on Lil, you open it," said Tom, holding Lucky Peanut. "He wants to have a look too."

I took the lid off. Underneath was some very thin brown Chinese newspaper. THERE WAS THE TREASURE BOX! And there was the green jade dragon disc inlaid on the top. A shiver ran down my spine. I lifted the box out and put it on the bottom bunk. It was made of dark wood with four rectangular sides. Each side had two panels inlaid with flower carvings.

Then we saw the Chinese lock fastening two panels together. I slipped the flat key into the grooves at the end of the lock and pushed.

"It fits!" we both cried out in surprise.

The lock unfastened into two pieces. I pulled gently at one of the panels, and simultaneously a panel opened on each side of the treasure box like a fan. Inside each fan compartment were tiny shelves full of miniature objects. Carefully, we took them out.

"Look! A yellow dog," said Tom in delight. "He's scowling."

"... and a white tiger!" I exclaimed. There was a green deer, which I thought was jade. Then I spotted the camel – moon white and perfectly carved. They were beautiful.

"Just think Tom," I said, "these are only copies. Somewhere in China the *real* works of art that look exactly like these are hidden away; the Emperors' treasures."

My favourite object was an amber stone carved in the shape of a curled leaf. In the centre was a tiny butterfly, so delicate I felt it might crumble in my hands.

"Just wait till we tell Mum," said Tom happily. "It's brilliant."

"It is," I said, but my heart was in turmoil. There were no directions. No writing to say where the real treasure could be hidden. I thought the box would give us some kind of sign for where to start looking.

I tossed and turned in bed that night, unable to sleep. I got up several times to examine each miniature inside the treasure box, but I couldn't find anything to help me. Nothing to give me hope.

No clue to trace the treasure I wanted to find so desperately. Mum was right. The secret of the Emperor's treasure had died with Grandpa Zhang, three hundred years ago.

Chapter Nine

A Fever

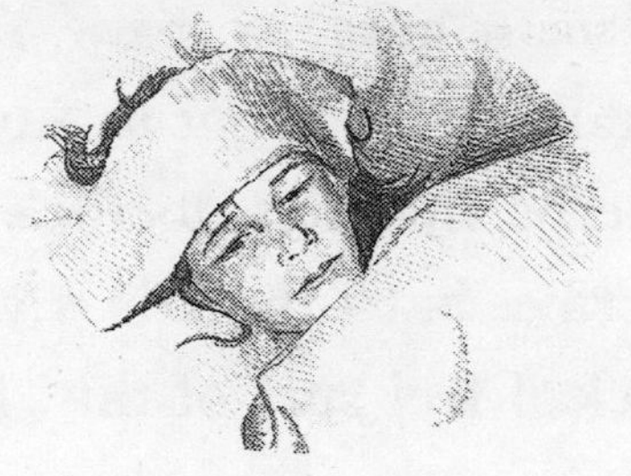

I SLEPT FITFULLY, and by morning I felt achy and hot. I had dreamt about the farm; of bulldozers tearing down the woods and hedges. I saw chemicals being sprayed on the fields, the rabbits dying and the wild flowers withering in front of me.

"Wake up Lil, you're screaming," said Tom, looking anxiously at me. I couldn't speak, and my head really hurt.

In between dreams I saw Aunt Li and Grandma sitting at my bedside, mopping my forehead. Sometimes I thought I saw my mother there, and I was apologising to her for not finding the treasure and saving the farm.

Grandma and Aunt Li brought me a cool, strange-tasting drink.

"Take sips, little sips," said Aunt Li.

Grandma held my clammy hand. "Bin Bin's Lily, you are so like your mother. Your emotions can be read from the wrinkles in your brow. You have a secret. I can see a great sorrow. You might feel better if you talk to me about it. Aunt Li will give you all the herbs that her doctor's teaching and learning prescribe, but I think it is your spirit that makes you sick. I feel sure of this. I haven't lived these eighty years not to have found some wisdom."

I nodded. "Thank you Grandma."

"When you are ready to tell us, we are here." She got up slowly to walk out of the room. Aunt Li tucked my blanket around me again.

"Where's Tom gone?" I asked.

"To visit the pandas. Our second cousin is a vet at the Breeding Research Base."

"Tom will love that," I muttered. I fell asleep again. This time it was a deep, restful sleep.

I woke up to find Tom sitting on the floor next to me, looking inside a red fortune wrapper.

"Look Lil, you've got one too," he said, seeing my eyes open. "You keep the money inside for luck. And it is lucky because Mum rang earlier to see how we were. She said Primrose has had her lambs; two of them. Rosa and Daisy." Before I had time to take in this news he continued. "Oh Lil, I wish you'd seen the pandas. A baby panda arrived while we were there. He'd been found wandering sick and hungry on one of the reserves. After Cousin Tsui gave him a bottle of milk, he scampered around us pulling at our trousers."

Tom picked up the treasure box as he spoke. The four compartments were still open. He took out each miniature and turned the treasure box upside-down. Then he started to shake it to make sure it was empty.

"Stop, you'll damage it!" I cried, when quite suddenly the jade dragon disc that was set into the top of the box fell out on to the bed.

"Tom!" I gasped. I picked it up and stared at it in disbelief.

"What is it, Lil? You look like you've seen a ghost."

"Writing Tom, look! Chinese writing!" I yelled in delight.

The underside of the jade disc was inscribed with Chinese characters.

Aunt Li and Grandma came rushing into the room, wondering at the noise.

"Look Aunt Li, Tom found it... some writing... it might be important. A clue."

"A clue to what?" asked Tom and Aunt Li together.

"To finding the hidden treasure of course. What did you all think?"

Aunt Li looked amazed. "Bin Bin's Lily, we cannot be sure that the treasure really exists. Some of the family thought Grandpa Zhang may have wanted to make a treasure box just to entertain his grandchildren. It's a nice story, but..."

"Please Aunt Li," I begged. "Just look at the characters. Can you read what it says?"

Aunt Li and Grandma looked at it and talked to each other earnestly.

"It is a poem," said Aunt Li at last. "We understand bits, but it needs a scholar of Chinese and English to translate it properly."

Tom was ecstatic. "Treasure and poems and pandas and fireworks," he chanted. "I must go and tell Cousin Tsui about this." And he dashed out of the room.

Aunt Li and Grandma were left looking at me.

"It's for Mum and Dad," I explained, babbling with excitement. "We must find the treasure to help save the farm. They've got no money left. Otherwise they'll lose everything and have to sell it to people who'll destroy it all. That's the real reason they couldn't come here. Mum didn't say because she didn't want you to worry. Tom doesn't know either. It is everything that we love. All the animals depend on us and now there's Primrose's lambs. That's why we must discover what the poem says."

Aunt Li sat down thoughtfully. "And of course our Bin Bin told us nothing of this when she rang today."

Grandma touched my forehead. She and Aunt Li spoke again. Aunt Li wiped her eyes and cleared her throat.

"I have a school friend who lives here in the city. He is a teacher of Chinese and English. He will be able to read it for us. I'm sure of that. If your fever is down, we will go to him tomorrow."

Chapter Ten
Qin

Qin, Aunt Li's friend, was slightly stooped and dressed in the blue overalls that had once been the Chinese people's uniform. He led us through several empty classrooms to his own tiny room. We sat down by his desk.

"I am overjoyed, Li, to help your niece and nephew. I have listened to the English-speaking BBC for years. In fact I am proud that my sister sold Yuen to buy me my radio."

"Who's Yuen?" I asked as politely as I could.

"Why, it was her best pig, of course."

He waved to his treasured, old-fashioned radio on a nearby shelf and smiled. He was so friendly and open, we felt we had known him for years. He hummed to himself as he got out a magnifying glass to get a clearer look at the characters on the jade disc. Very carefully, he began to copy them on to a piece of paper.

Tom was now sitting on the desk, peering over Qin's skinny shoulder. "Chinese characters look a bit like a bird's footsteps," he said slowly.

"That's a wise thought, Tom," said Qin. "There is a legend that Cang Jie, a mythical Emperor, devised our characters from the tracks of birds and animals."

Qin's face grew serious as he concentrated. He got out several dictionaries and sniffed a few times.

As he began to translate the poem, he spoke each word slowly and carefully. In those words he unfolded a greater source of hope than I could ever have imagined.

"*In the land of the green gauze belt and the blue jade hairpins*," began Qin.

"Well, that doesn't make sense, does it?" said Tom, disappointed.

"Yes it does!" exclaimed Aunt Li. "It is from an ancient poem I was taught at school."

A light of recognition stirred in Qin's face. "Of course, I remember now!"

"It's referring to Yangshuo in Guangxi province – a beautiful part of China." Aunt Li paced up and down the tiny room as she spoke. "The green gauze belt is the river and the blue jade hairpins are those *shihuishi maoyan* mountains. Qin, how do you say that?"

"Peaks, I believe."

"Yes, yes, thank you, and these... peaks seem to rise out of the water."

"This is a school," exclaimed Qin. "We must have a map somewhere to show these two." He rushed into a neighbouring classroom and came back with a dusty old atlas. "There we are, Yangshuo and the River Lijang," he said, pointing to a river that snaked through many peaks.

"Now back to work," said Qin, and he continued to translate. "*Lights on the river in...*" He paused for a moment. "*... the lingering dusk. And cormorants... dive in the pools.*"

"Is this still part of your ancient poem?" I asked Aunt Li.

"No, no, this is new."

"Oh! Please continue," I begged Qin. "I didn't mean to interrupt."

"*Beyond where tigers sleep and the grey owl flew...* no," he corrected himself, "*glides. Lie gates to...*" He paused again. "*Lie gates to a palace in the path of buffaloes.*"

"A palace!" I gasped. In my mind I already saw gleaming golden rooftops nestled between tall limestone mountains.

"And buffaloes – so mysterious," sighed Tom.

"Qin," said Aunt Li, impatient with excitement, "we've interrupted you again. There is more, isn't there?"

"One last bit," he answered. "*From earth's harvest to the sun where weaves a lizard's tail. Let they who have knowledge...* no, no... *wisdom, find the path.*"

"Find the path," repeated Tom in awe. "Lily,

what does it mean? Could it be to the treasure, the path to the treasure?" He was shouting now.

"Yes. Yes. I think so," Qin laughed. "And the rest of the lines are like..."

"SIGNS," I cried out. "Clues leading us to the treasure."

"Goodness, Bin Bin's Lily!" said Aunt Li. Her cheeks were flushed and she was gathering her bags together. "You were right to take Grandpa Zhang's story seriously. Thank you Qin. There is no time to be lost, my holiday from the hospital will be over soon. We must tell Grandma Tsui that we are leaving for Yangshuo in the morning!"

She gave Qin a hug. Then they both looked at their feet. Qin cleared his throat.

"Right," said Aunt Li, and stepped out into the crowded Chengdu street.

"If we find the treasure," pronounced Tom, "we'll get a lap-top each, Qin, and then we can e-mail each other. I'll tell you all about the new lambs."

"I'll look forward to that," said Qin, waving as Aunt Li and I pulled Tom on to the waiting bus.

I was determined to make Tom's promise come true.

CHAPTER ELEVEN

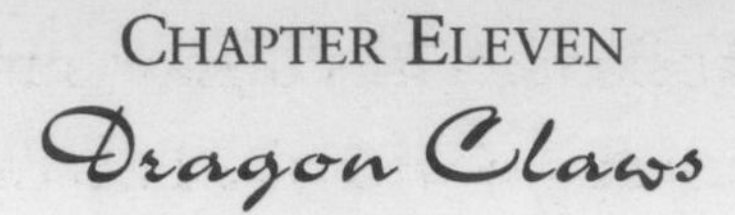

TOM LEANED OUT of his bunk above me and drew on the steamed-up carriage window. Once again we were hurtling across China on a very long train journey.

"There!" said Tom, finishing his picture.

"What is it?" I asked.

"It's a cormorant of course!" he exclaimed.

"Yes, Bin Bin's children!" came Aunt Li's voice from the sleeper bunk below. "I must tell you."

"What, Aunt Li?" said Tom and I, peering, upside-down, over the edge of our bunks. She had her slippers on, a blow-up neck cushion, a hot water bottle and a pile of books next to her.

"Grandma Tsui and I spoke last night about the poem. She remembered the cormorant fishermen. They go out on the Lijang river with boats and wide wicker baskets. The cormorants dive for fish which they then share with the fishermen."

"Just like the poem says," said Tom. "*Where cormorants dive in the pools.*"

"Do they still fish that way?" I asked. "I mean, are they still there?"

"Indeed," said Aunt Li. "Some things haven't changed in China for hundreds of years."

At that moment a train official arrived with a kettle to fill our cups with tea. When she'd gone I said:

"Aunt Li, maybe the fishermen will be able to give us some idea of where to start. Maybe they'd know where tigers sleep and then we could search for the palace."

"You read my mind, Lily Dragon," laughed Aunt Li.

"I'm hoping to find a home for Lucky Peanut," muttered Tom. "It should be warmer there."

It was much warmer, but pouring with rain, as we stepped on to the river ferry that would take us to Yangshuo. It was such a novelty to feel warm that Tom and I sat with our feet dangling off the edge of the boat. We let the rain soak us to the skin. Aunt Li sat with the other passengers under an awning, shaking her head.

The rain cleared and we watched the mountains slowly emerging out of the mist that still clothed the riverbank.

"The hairpin mountains," said Aunt Li in delight.

Some children, who were washing clothes in the river, waved to us.

"Look at the buffalo," I said in amazement.

Farmers were ploughing a field using buffalo to pull the plough. I thought of Dad waving to us from the tractor as we left for China. Mother had said that the sale of the farm would be at the end of the month. We only had a week to go. A week to find the treasure. I wondered if it was long enough.

In Yangshuo, Tom made friends with a lady who was carving name seals outside our hostel. In broken English she told us about a special restaurant where we could choose our own food and watch it being cooked.

"There's snake, dog and even dragon claws," said Tom, full of bravado.

"Dragon claws, Tom!" I laughed. "She's pulling your leg."

"Well the snake and dog are true," said Tom defiantly.

When it came to it, we both chose egg, vegetables and rice for supper, and some lychees to kccp for later. Aunt Li asked for snake, and then got deep in conversation with one of the cooks.

"I asked about a palace in the area," she explained when she joined us with the food. "Whether there was one or had ever been one in this area. It is just as I thought. No one has any knowledge... or if they have," she said quietly, "they don't like to mention it."

"Why?" asked Tom.

"Most of our palaces were destroyed during the Cultural Revolution or at the beginning of the century. People want to forget. But if we eat quickly..." said Aunt Li, brightening. She began to wolf down her snake and rice as fast as she could. Then she paused. "Bin Bin's children, eat up – why are you staring at me?" She began her sentence again. "They say that the cormorant fishermen are still on the river as dusk falls, down by the bridge on the way to Moon Hill. If we eat quickly, we can hire *zixingxhe* across the road."

"Bicycles," said Tom triumphantly before I could translate. "See! I'm learning."

"Then Tom," said Aunt Li, "you and Lily may go and hire the bicycles, while I finish my supper. Don't forget to get one for me."

"Do you think Mum ever ate snake?" asked Tom, as we pedalled out of town following Aunt Li.

"I don't know, but it certainly makes Aunt Li

very speedy," I said breathlessly as Aunt Li zoomed ahead of us on her rickety old bicycle. I swerved to avoid the people crossing the road in front of us.

The dusk made the mountains into fantastic shapes. Ahead of us, on the misty river, were the silhouettes of fishermen. They wore coolie hats, and I could just make out the silhouettes of the cormorants perched precariously on their thin rafts.

Each boat had a lantern at its stern, hanging above the river and casting a pool of light over the water. I stopped my bike and stood very still.

"Come on, Lil!" shouted Tom.

"*Lights on the river in the lingering dusk*," I whispered. "Aunt Li! Tom!" I was running now. "The second line of the poem – *lights on the river*! Look! This must be what Grandpa Zhang meant!"

Chapter Twelve

"Sit Atop the Mountain and Watch the Tigers Fight"

Chinese Proverb

There was a small group of fishing boats moored to the riverbank. Tom offered the fishermen some of his lychees. They accepted enthusiastically, chatting and thanking him. Aunt Li seized the opportunity to ask them if they knew where the tigers sleep. For a minute they looked astonished. Then they burst into wheezy laughter and spat into the river.

I could see that the general mirth began to irritate Aunt Li, who became agitated. Her expression was very severe, and from the tone of her next speech, I guessed she was demanding a sensible answer. The fishermen, now reprimanded, talked amongst themselves earnestly. There was more spitting. One of them shrugged his shoulders and spoke.

"We know nothing of a sleeping tiger," translated Aunt Li. "No tigers around here."

"You could tell them it's from an old poem," I suggested.

This time the fishermen pointed further downstream to a tiny speck of light.

"They say that Lin Bao is further down the river. If anyone knows, it will be him."

It was now completely dark. We slipped and bumped in the weak light of the cycle lamps as we tried to follow the track that ran alongside the riverbank. It was almost half a mile to where Lin Bao's boat was moored.

A dignified old man was sitting on a wooden crate beside the boat. He did not turn his head, or answer as Aunt Li called out a greeting. We walked into the glow of his lantern. He was using a small knife to whittle away at a piece of wood.

"*Nihao*," Aunt Li tried again.

He answered in a crabby voice. Aunt Li translated for us: "He purposefully moved out here to have peace and hopes we have a good reason for disturbing him."

"Sorry," I said in Chinese, remembering how much I loved sitting alone on the hill above the farm.

He looked up and his face softened. He pulled over a little bench. We all three sat down and Aunt Li explained our reason for coming. He nodded vigorously, put down his carving and spoke. He smiled at Tom and me, whilst Aunt Li translated.

"My grandfather told me the myth of the Sleeping Tiger. Back in ancient times, when the stars weren't fixed in the heavens, the tiger fought with the bear. Too clever and cunning, the tiger triumphed over the bear. The bear retreated to the farthest corner of our universe. The tiger, exhausted by the fight, fell asleep on the mountain top. He has been there ever since. A few of us old ones wait for the day when he awakes."

"But how can we find him?" I asked.

He listened to Aunt Li translating my words.

"Look." He pointed triumphantly, but all I could see was the blackness of the night sky. Puzzled, I stared at him.

"I am foolish," he said. "We must move away from the lantern." Taking our hands in his, he moved, suddenly youthful in his enthusiasm, to the riverbank. Our eyes took a while to adjust, and then he pointed to the shadowy silhouette of a mountain. There at the top, in a pattern of stars, lay the sleeping tiger.

I'd never seen stars shine so brilliantly before. We gazed at the tiger.

"Of course Grandpa Zhang knew that the sleeping tiger could only be seen when it was dark, when there were lights on the river," exclaimed Aunt Li.

"Have you ever been beyond Sleeping Tiger Mountain?" I asked Lin Bao. "Do you know what we would find there?"

Lin Bao shook his head. "I have never been, I've never had reason to go. Probably more farms and people like me trying to make ends meet."

"Would you ever take us down the river to the mountain?" I asked, desperate now to begin our search. "Tomorrow, I mean."

"I will," said Aunt Li, translating Lin Bao's answer, "but you must come early. I've got a day's fishing to do when I return."

"*Xiexie ni*," said Tom, "thank you."

Then, ignoring Aunt Li's protestations, Lin Bao led us back through the paddy fields, to the road and to Moon Hill bridge. Without a goodbye he set off back into the darkness. Our feet were soaking, but we were filled with the fervour and excitement of adventure.

Maybe Lin Bao is the spirit of Grandpa Zhang, I thought, after he left. He's come back to help us find the treasure.

Yangshuo was still thronging with people when we returned. Aunt Li explained to the hostel owner that we were going off to travel in the mountains for a day or so, but that we would like to leave our luggage.

"Aren't you afraid?" she asked in English, as she looked worriedly at Tom and me.

Aunt Li looked startled. "Should we be afraid?" she asked.

"Are there dangerous animals?" said Tom, his eyes widening.

"No... well, perhaps snakes."

"Why do you ask then?" I said, curious now.

The lady looked confused. "People from here don't go over the mountain. Take lots of food and water and be watchful."

This hint of danger only added to the mystery of the unknown journey that lay before us. Aunt Li bustled about, Tom looked deep in thought and I felt intoxicated with excitement and hope.

"Maybe," said Tom as we packed our rucksacks, "there are wolves or bears out there that she doesn't want to tell us about."

"Don't be stupid," I said, throwing my sponge at him.

"We will need water bottles, saucepan, bedrolls," said Aunt Li checking her list and ignoring Tom's remark. "It's late but I'll go and see what I can find."

"All the same, I've put in matches," said Tom. "We'll keep the fire burning at night, just in case."

Chapter Thirteen

Sleeping Tiger Mountain

I HAD PUT the alarm clock under my pillow so that I wouldn't sleep through the alarm. Grandpa Zhang's poem was tucked into the pocket of my shirt. Tom was already dressed when we woke him.

"Thought I'd wear today's clothes instead of my pyjamas so I'd be ready," he explained.

We helped each other on with our rucksacks. Aunt Li had fixed a bedroll and a tin water bottle on to each of them. She had a saucepan dangling next to her water bottle. They drummed against each other, announcing our little convoy as we cycled through the crowds of villagers on the early morning streets.

"Wait," said Aunt Li as we passed the market. "We need food."

She haggled and argued at several stalls, packing

vegetables, fruit and bread into her rucksack. We ate some bread for breakfast and climbed back on to our bikes for our big adventure.

As we cycled out of town into the countryside, a haze of pink morning sky floated just above the river and clung to chosen rocks and trees.

Once, a couple of years back, Mum had made Tom and me a Chinese garden for New Year. It was a huge bowl with rocks and plants growing inside it. There was a mirror lake and some tiny pottery Chinese figures: a man sitting cross-legged with a spindly fishing rod, a horse and cart and a figure herding a collection of ducks with a long stick. Now it was as though our Chinese garden had come to life.

When we reached Moon Hill bridge we could see Lin Bao's hut in the distance. He waved us on to his boat and wheeled our bikes to his shed. A moment later he had joined us and was casting off. Aunt Li handed him some bread, but he held up a strip of dried fish and enthusiastically took a bite. Tom took the oars with Lin Bao and helped to heave them backwards and forwards. I looked up from the river, towards the distant mountains, hoping that the sleeping tiger might reveal its three-hundred-year-old secret to us.

My thoughts were interrupted by a chirrup. Then I noticed a box, on the bench next to Tom.

"Tom! You haven't brought Lucky Peanut with you, have you?" I exclaimed.

"Of course, Lil. I thought he might like to live on Sleeping Tiger Mountain. Anyway, I couldn't leave him behind. I didn't know when we'd be back."

And so, passing in and out of the river mist, we floated slowly down the Lijang.

Lin Bao turned the boat down a tributary river. It was yet another couple of miles before he pulled into the shore.

"This path," he explained to Aunt Li, "is what you must follow to your mountain."

He helped us off the boat. When I looked up to thank him, he'd already turned and was rowing back along the river. "*Xiexie ni*," I called out, as his boat was swallowed up in the mist.

I ran after Tom. He had set off along the dirt path that wended its way through a tapestry of brilliant emerald green fields. It was a moment of dreams and hope that I would never forget. Aunt Li hummed cheerfully as we walked, and told us stories of when she and Mum were little.

"Then there was the time when I was looking

after Bin Bin and she found a pair of scissors. She cut the mandarin ducks off your Grandma's best slippers. How I was scolded!"

Gradually, the path led us into the trees at the foot of Sleeping Tiger Mountain. Less formidable now, the mountain was cloaked in green and lit up by the early morning sunshine. We scrambled up the lower slopes, high enough to watch the watery rice fields turn to glass.

We ate our lunch in the afternoon sun, under a rock shelf.

"This has got to be the perfect spot for him," announced Tom.

"For who?" I said dozily, resting my tired feet on my rucksack.

"For Lucky, of course! Imagine – he was cooped up in a cage in that dark little shop in the city and now he can begin a new life amongst the ferns. He's got camouflage and friends. I can hear them."

He opened the box and set the little cricket free into the warm sunshine. "There you go Lucky. We'll miss you."

Aunt Li looked at Tom proudly.

"Well done Bin Bin's Tom, we have at least accomplished the first part of our mission. We mustn't rest too long. We must hurry on before night starts to fall."

At times the woods flanking the mountainside became so dense that the only way forward was to climb higher and higher. In amongst the pine trees the ground was criss-crossed with roots and ferns. Each bend in the mountain promised to be the last. But as we tramped deeper into the trees, there seemed to be no end to the twists and turns between us and the valley beyond. Somewhere off in the distance a dog barked.

"Bin Bin's children, I wish I had your stamina," said Aunt Li, flagging a little for the first time. She laughed and scolded us as in a fit of energy Tom and I jumped and ran wildly between the trees. We were going downhill. With the momentum of the slope, we almost lost control of our feet.

Tom was ahead of me, and then I saw what he hadn't noticed in the darkened shadows. We were racing towards a sheer and sudden drop.

"Tom!" I screamed. "Tom, STOP! There's a cliff!"

Tom had disappeared behind a rock. I scrambled down and saw him clutching tightly to a tree root to break his fall.

I held on to him as Aunt Li came up behind us calling in Chinese. She threw her arms around us in relief.

"Thank heavens! Thank heavens you are both safe."

"Let's look over," said Tom mischievously.

"On your hands and knees," ordered Aunt Li.

The three of us wriggled out of our rucksacks and crawled on all fours to the edge of the precipice. We gazed down at the stark dramatic drop below us.

"It's no use," sighed Aunt Li. "We'll have to go back."

Our hearts sank at this thought.

"But Aunt Li, we've come so far," said Tom.

"I'm sure the valley is just beyond this last slope."

"I'm sure too Tom, but what choice have we got? There seems to be no way through these trees. We'll go back quickly before night comes and find a place to sleep. Tomorrow we can go down to the rice fields and walk around the base of the mountain."

We lay quite still, gazing hopelessly at the drop below. A purple sky announced that dusk was creeping up on us. There was a flurry of wings and something sailed over our heads, making us jump. It took off down the mountainside to our right, making a deep hooting call as it passed.

"An owl," cried Tom. "Just as Grandpa Zhang said! *Where the grey owl glides.*"

Watching the owl sail away gave me an idea.

"Aunt Li, wait! We could walk down through the trees to the right. Follow the way the owl went. Surely we'd come out at the bottom of the cliff and then we could walk across this last slope? It would save going back."

"Lily Dragon, that would be reckless. There could be another precipice below, and in this dusk we might miss it. Just because Grandpa Zhang's poem mentions an owl doesn't mean we start following one off a cliff."

"Let's try, Aunt Li," I pleaded. "If we're wrong we can just come back up and sleep here."

"Come on Aunt Li," said Tom, who had already set off down the steep bank to our right. "You're our bravest aunt."

"I'm your only aunt," she said grumbling, but she set off reluctantly after us. "What would Bin Bin think of me getting you out here on this wild mountainside?"

We were silent now, steadying ourselves on branches and tree trunks. We had to pick out every detail of the slope ahead. Then we reached a patch of ground that was strangely smooth. It snaked ahead of us. We followed it until Aunt Li let out a funny cry.

"Great heavens, Bin Bin's children, it's a PATH... How clever you are. You have found a path!"

Chapter Fourteen

"Beyond where Tigers Sleep and the Grey Owl Glides"

Grandpa Zhang

IT WAS DARK, but a huge full moon lit up the mountainside. We followed the path on to the rocky escarpment below the cliff. Hope gave us energy. The clang of the water bottle and saucepan on Aunt Li's rucksack echoed rhythmically. For a moment I could imagine we were a royal Chinese party on our way to a nearby summer palace.

Steps, roughly hewn into the rocks, led us back into the trees. The path turned a last corner, and there before us lay a deep blue valley. Distant limestone mountains were glorious in the moonlight. An inky river meandered before us, and below we could see buildings – a tiny village huddled under sloping roofs.

Tom's hand slipped into mine as we gazed down, disappointment resting upon us.

"Didn't you..." said Tom, "... didn't you think we might find a palace here, Aunt Li?"

"Well of course not," said Aunt Li, trying to be realistic. "Had there been a palace we would have been told. No... Well, perhaps I did hope, but a village is good news – fresh water, and beds if I ask the right way."

Even that hope faded as we drew nearer to the village, for it became clear that it was abandoned. Aunt Li took out a small lantern from her rucksack and we peered into empty, crumbling stone cottages. Sometimes a table had been left behind, or a stool.

"In here," sighed Aunt Li, "this will do. We'll sleep here tonight."

There was a terrible scuttling noise that made my flesh creep.

"Ugh, rats!" said Tom and I in disgust.

Aunt Li looked at us in surprise. "As farmers' children you should know that a rat is a promising sign, one of prosperity. Where there are rats there is plenty of food. We are happy for our children to be born in the Year of the Rat!"

Prosperity or not, Tom and I made sure that we

chased the rats away before we put our bedrolls on the dusty floor. Using broken pieces of wood taken from a table, we built a fire in the hearth. Aunt Li bustled about and cooked us a supper of vegetables and rice in a strange-tasting sauce. After all our walking, we ate ravenously. It was quite a cold night and we moved our bedrolls near the hearth.

"Tom," I called, "what time is it at home?"

There was no reply. He had already fallen asleep, exhausted from our journey. I missed Mum and Dad terribly that night. Maybe it was because the hope of finding Grandpa Zhang's treasure seemed more remote than ever.

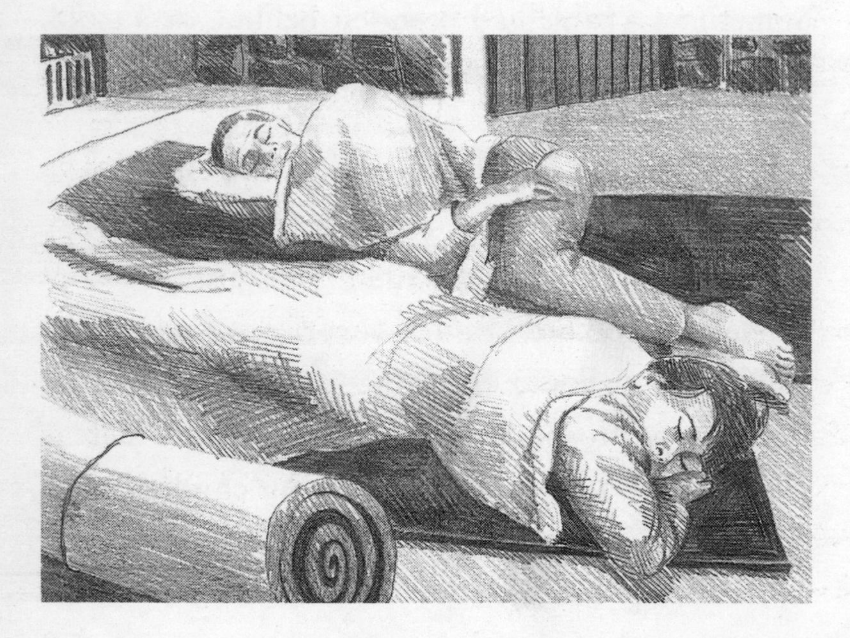

I woke up with a start. Dusty sunlight shone on Tom's empty bedroll next to me. Aunt Li was still fast asleep, curled up under her jumpers. The room smelt of spices and smoky warmth from the embers in the hearth. Yesterday's clothes felt uncomfortable. I took off my socks and headed out of the house into narrow cobbled paths. I delighted in the feeling of the cold stone on my bare feet. We must have slept late, as the sun was almost above me as I walked.

"Tom!" I shouted, my English voice an unfamiliar echo on these Chinese walls.

"Over here, Lil!"

Tom had found a courtyard with a small stone hut at its centre. The hut had sloping roofs with pillars and a wall that came up to my waist. Tom was sitting on the wall throwing stones.

"Look Lil, if you get some stones you can sit up on this ledge like me and then you can throw them. If you aim just right you can get them through the wooden slats into the well. I've got seven out of seven!"

Below us was a large, circular latticed lid. A cover to a well. The stones made a satisfying clatter before they dropped through the gaps.

A shrill cry and a strange bellowing interrupted our game.

"Tom, Lily Dragon, come quickly!" called Aunt Li.

We dropped our stones and scrambled down from the wall. We ran to where Aunt Li was standing, outside our temporary home, looking over the valley. A small herd of buffalo, driven by a young boy, was lumbering slowly through the fields around the village and down in the direction of the river.

Chapter Fifteen
Sang

THE YOUNG BOY was amazed as we emerged from the village and set off down the slope towards him. He stepped behind the first buffalo and peeped shyly out. Aunt Li started talking to reassure him, and gradually he smiled.

"He is Sang," translated Aunt Li. "He apologises because he doesn't often see strangers."

We joined him at the front of the procession and walked with him to the river. Every time the buffalo behind us snorted, its warm breath tickled my back. Aunt Li translated our conversation.

"Where have you come from?" he asked.

Aunt Li explained that she was from Beijing and that we lived in England. His face lit up and he nodded. He thought for a moment and said something to Aunt Li.

"Big Ben," translated Aunt Li.

"Yes, that's right," said Tom, imitating the chimes and surprising the buffalo. "Do you come from this village?"

"We used to," said Sang, "but we were moved. All our families were, up the valley to a co-operative farm."

"Why do you come back then?" I asked.

"For the buffalo. Once a week I take them to wallow in the Golden Water."

"The Golden Water?" said Aunt Li curiously.

"We have a river nearer to us, but we believe that the Golden Water here gives them a long and healthy life."

"And have the buffalo always taken this path to the Golden Water?" asked Aunt Li.

The boy nodded. "Well, all my life anyway."

I knew what Aunt Li was thinking. This might be *the path of buffaloes* that Grandpa Zhang included in his poem. However, this would have to be a tradition of three hundred years, and Sang couldn't be more than ten years old.

With a lot of snuffling and nudging, the buffalo waded into the river. Tom and I joined them, washing our faces in the cool water and splashing each other. Sang and Aunt Li stayed on the riverbank. I heard her mumbling Grandpa Zhang's poem quietly to herself in Chinese. She looked off into the distance, repeating, "*gates to a palace in the path of buffaloes*," over and over again. I saw Sang look up and say something to her in Chinese. They spoke rapidly back and forth to each other. Aunt Li looked increasingly surprised.

"What's he saying Aunt Li? What's he saying?"

"He heard me mention a palace, and I told him our journey was following the lines of an ancient poem. He said there was a story he'd heard that there hadn't always been a village here on the hill. That on the side of the Golden Water there had stood a magnificent palace."

Sang smiled and added something more. Aunt Li's face fell as she explained that Sang thought it might all be a folk tale.

I wanted to start looking for traces of this palace straightaway. But after we had said goodbye to Sang, Aunt Li made sure we ate some more of her left-over vegetables and rice.

Finally, we began our search. There was no pattern to it. We scrambled over rocks, in and out of houses, looking under ancient rusty corrugated iron roofs, searching in weedy patches, all desperate for any sign through that long, hot afternoon. At last, filthy and exhausted, we had to acknowledge to each other that there was nothing to betray a palace. Nothing to give us any hope. It was Aunt Li who voiced our desperation. Her bustling demeanour was cast aside.

"All just myths and fairy tales," she sighed as she wiped her face. "Every clue we've followed is only guesswork. Nothing tangible. It's no use. Let's go and wash in the river."

"But there's the next line in Grandpa Zhang's poem, Aunt Li," I said desperately. "We haven't even thought about that yet."

"You are right Lily, we'll sit and work on it tonight."

But we all knew that this line, *from earth's harvest to the sun where weaves a lizard's tail*, was the most mystifying of all.

Then the greatest twist of fate occurred. As Tom took off his shorts to wade in the river, a piece of paper fell out on to a tuft of rice grass. I picked it up. Tom looked very guilty.

"Aunt Li..."

"What, Bin Bin's Tom, what? You look like

you've stepped on a snake." She was teasing now.

"No, Aunt Li," said Tom very seriously. "The hostel lady gave me this bit of paper for you as we left Yangshuo yesterday. I stuffed it in my pocket. I forgot all about it."

Aunt Li laughed. "It's probably a receipt for our luggage."

But it wasn't.

"Bin Bin's children, I am so sorry!" cried Aunt Li.

What Aunt Li, what's happened?" I said, alarmed.

"We will have to leave. The hospital needs me back immediately. I am to fly back to Beijing just as soon as I return you to Grandma in Chengdu."

"But Aunt Li!" said Tom, "not yet! We've got to look at the next line of the poem. We could be close to the treasure now."

"No Tom, you don't understand. We have to leave in the morning. If the hospital want me, I have no choice. I shall try to come back to Chengdu as soon as I can and maybe, before your holiday is up, we'll come back. We could even bring someone with us, talk to a guide, get proper help."

I followed Aunt Li back up the path to the village.

"Aunt Li," I pleaded. "You've forgotten the farm. We've only got a few days now. The sale will go through and it'll be too late. Mum and Dad will lose everything. We're so close. How can we give up now?"

"I haven't forgotten, Lily Dragon, but it is out of my hands. We'll ring Bin Bin and tell her what we know. Maybe they can hold the sale back by a few weeks. Now Lily, go back to Tom and wash and we'll eat tonight by the river."

I couldn't believe what Aunt Li was saying. She couldn't understand what was at stake or how things worked where we came from, any more than I could understand why she had to return to Beijing. Myths and folk tales were all we had to find the treasure, but we couldn't ignore them. They were our last hope.

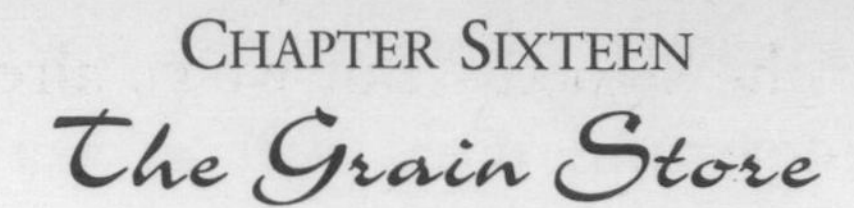

I FELT AUNT Li touch my forehead tenderly. I wanted to tell her my plan, but she would have had no choice but to stop us. Once she was asleep I would wake Tom. I was Lily Dragon now, strong and brave, but deep in my heart I was terribly afraid.

I must have slept too, because when I woke, the fire in the hearth had gone out. I rolled over to Tom and cupped my hand over his mouth. I leaned close and whispered in his ear:

"Tom, listen to me. Take that rucksack and follow me."

We crept out of the house. Aunt Li stirred once, but we made it into the moonlit path outside.

"What Lil? What's happening?" asked Tom sleepily.

"We've got to search, Tom. We've got to."

"OK Lil," he sighed. "But we've already looked everywhere."

"No Tom, you don't understand. Just as we went to sleep I had an idea. The *well*... When we threw those stones there were no splashes, were there?"

"No Lil, but..."

"So we must look then. That well could have been there for hundreds of years."

"But Lil," said Tom, more awake now, "it's not a well. Aunt Li told me, it's an old grain store."

"Tom!" I was clutching his arm so hard that he cried out. "Why didn't you say?"

"I didn't think it was important."

"But Tom, that's it!"

"What?"

"A grain store, a place they store rice or wheat. Maybe that's what Grandpa Zhang meant by *earth's harvest*."

The crickets in the trees around us seemed to be singing with high-pitched excitement as we put our lantern down next to the grain store. In silent understanding we each held on to one side of the wooden lid and carefully, very carefully, managed to lift it out of our way. Tom took the lantern and held it down into the dark hollow.

"Look! Aunt Li was right," I whispered. It was about three metres deep, lined with stone slabs and there at the bottom we could just see the scattered remains of rice grain.

"I'm going down," I said to Tom. "I've got to get a closer look."

"But Lil..." began Tom.

"It's OK, Tom. Look, there are metal rods hammered into the stone in places. I'll climb down on those ones there and then jump. When I'm down you attach the lantern to the rucksack. We'll undo the strap and then you can lower it down to me."

First one foot, then the other, and then my hands and I jumped. The old grain and dirt cushioned my fall. When I walked, some of the stones we'd thrown down the day before dug into my feet. I cried out.

"Lily, are you OK?" Tom's face, lit up like a Hallowe'en pumpkin, gazed anxiously down at me.

"I'm fine, wait a minute... Now pass down the lantern."

He lowered it down to me. "What's there, Lil?" he whispered. "Can you see anything?"

"No Tom, nothing. I'll try and dig up some of this stuff that's under my feet." With the lantern in one hand I started to push the rice, dirt and stones to one side.

"Hang on Lil, I'm coming," said Tom. He climbed down.

"Here... Tom!" I'd uncovered a curious ring stuck in the ground.

"It's only mud around it, Lil. It's not stuck."

We dug at it, and it lifted.

"It's a handle," said Tom, hoarse with excitement.

"Look, move to one side, Tom."

I crouched down a distance from the handle and pulled. Something stirred. Tom helped me. We pulled again and cracks began to form in the mud and grain stuck to the stone floor.

"Again, Lily!"

We pulled it with all our strength, the weight making my heart beat faster.

"Once more," said Tom, and then we were thrown backwards as a slab of stone suddenly swung away from the floor. It was a trap door.

"Come on Lil!" cried Tom, and without a second thought, he took the lantern and dropped into the strange tunnel that ran beneath us.

It was like a mine-shaft I'd once seen in a book. We had to move along on our hands and knees. It felt suddenly cool and the air smelt of damp earth. It took me a while to get used to it and to be able to breathe freely. After a few minutes we found ourselves in a wider tunnel where we could stand. We crept on. The walls were still stone slabs, nothing to betray where we were.

"Look Tom, the tunnel's changing."

We'd arrived in a chamber, a circular room with passages going off it.

"How weird," said Tom, spinning around. "One, two, three, four, five, six, seven, eight tunnels."

"Which way now?" I said, bewildered.

"Let's try this one," said Tom, pointing straight ahead and setting off.

My stomach turned because I realised that I couldn't even remember which tunnel we'd just come from.

"Tom, Tom, stop. Look! Do you know which tunnel we just came out of?"

It was his turn to look shocked. "No Lily, I don't... they all look the same." He clutched my hand. "Are we lost?"

We found ourselves back in a passageway just like the first one. We walked, it seemed for ages, a nagging fear enveloping me.

"Look Lil, it's ending," cried Tom in delight. "It's OK."

But to our dismay we found ourselves back in the chamber with the eight tunnels.

"Let's try here," I said desperately now.

Again we walked, even ran, for what seemed like an eternity and found ourselves back in the same chamber again.

"It's like a maze, Tom – it's some strange maze."

"I'm *tired*," sighed Tom. "Can we stop a minute?"

We sat down and Tom held on to my arm. I thought of our warm, cosy kitchen at home and wondered if we would ever see it again.

"Lil, what do you think Mum and Dad are

doing now?" said Tom, breaking the silence.

"If I tell you Tom, you'll understand why I got you up. Why I had to look once more."

"Why, Lil?"

I explained it all, about the farm, how Mum and Dad were ill with worry and how the animals would no longer have a home.

"I thought if we could find the treasure we could save everything, but I was wrong. We're lost. I've got you into this mess and we'll only worry Mum and Dad more if they hear that we're lost."

Tom didn't say anything for a while. "I think you were right," he said finally. "At least Lucky's got a home in the wild now and maybe if we put something at the entrance of each tunnel as we go down it, we'll be able to find where we came in… Lil, can I just sleep though, for a little while? I'm very tired." He lay next to me with his head on the rucksack.

"I'll turn out the lantern Tom, to save the batteries."

I sat there in the darkness. I felt numb, a terrible cold feeling. I had to think. *From earth's harvest to the sun, where weaves a lizard's tail.* I said it over and over again. Something worried at me. If we were going from *earth's harvest to the sun*, we'd have to go upwards towards the outside. And yet here we were, stuck underground in the darkness. Logic told me that we had probably just stumbled on an old tunnel that had nothing to do with Grandpa Zhang, but that thought was too terrible to dwell on.

I turned the lantern on again. I had to have a drink of water, my throat was so dry – but I saw it was impossible to get the flask as Tom's head was on the rucksack. The lantern lit up in relief the doodle I'd drawn in the dust. It was a picture of the sun. I traced over it again now that it was light. A circle... the rays.

Then it hit me. The truth had been staring us in the face all this time.

"Tom, Tom!" I shook him. "Tom, *this is the sun!* Tom, we're sitting in it, Grandpa Zhang's sun. Look! The chamber is a circle and the tunnels are the rays. We've found it!"

We really *had* come from earth's harvest and found our way to the sun.

"*Where weaves a lizard's tail*," I whispered. "One of the tunnels must take us to the treasure, and *lizard's tail* must be the link... But how?"

"A lizard's tail is pointy, a bit like an arrow Lil," suggested Tom. "Perhaps there's one under all this dirt. I'll brush the floor with my rucksack to try and find it."

I checked the walls, the floor. We worked our way around each entrance.

"Nothing, Tom. Really nothing."

"What about this bit of rock, Lil?" said Tom. "It looks a bit like a lizard's tail." He went to grab at it, and it crumbled in his hands.

Tom was crouching near the lantern in the entrance to one of the tunnels. It was lit up like an exotic grotto. Something caught my eye. Tom was looking at it as well.

"It's not a crack, is it Lil?" said Tom. "It looks like writing."

Very faint, but painted into the stone, were some Chinese characters. They were almost too worn to make out but one looked familiar.

"I wish we had Aunt Li here," I said. "She'd be able to read it."

"I've seen it before," said Tom. "I remember thinking that it looked like two eyes and a smiling mouth... when Qin was translating the poem."

The poem was still in my pocket. I got it out and

we held it into the light, searching for the two eyes and the mouth.

"LIL, LOOK!" Tom was shouting now. "IT'S A *TAIL*! It's the second character in tail. Lizard's tail. This must be the tunnel!"

Chapter Seventeen
The Rock Fall

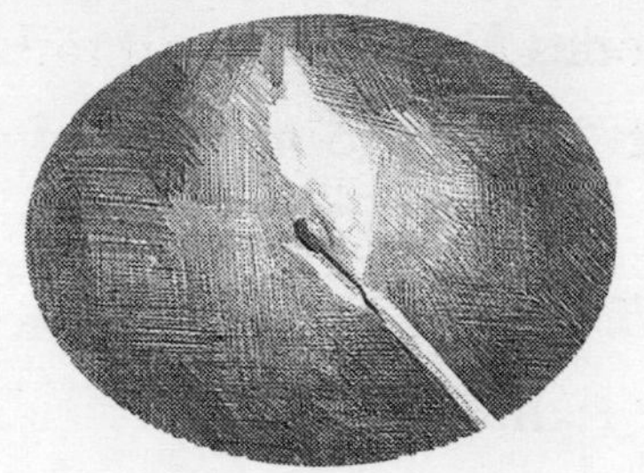

OUR SHADOWS WERE our only companions in this empty tunnel.

"Now I know what it felt like to be thrown in the dungeons," muttered Tom.

He was excited, it was all a game to him. But I was getting scared. Doubt was creeping into my thoughts, filling me with apprehension.

"I hope we're the first, Tom. The first to tread in Grandpa Zhang's steps. I hope the grain store was never emptied before. What if someone had already found the trap door?"

"Even if they had Lil, they wouldn't have had the poem so they'd have probably got lost in the maze. We might even stumble on their skeletons," said Tom cheerfully.

He turned around suddenly with the lamp under

his chin. His terrifying face made me jump. Laughing, I ran to grab him – and then we both faltered, horrified, because we saw we were approaching a dead end.

"It can't be!" I cried out. "The tunnel can't end here!"

"But the *lizard's tail*!" exclaimed Tom. "We *must* be in the right place."

He walked up to the wall of stone and leaned against it despondently.

"Tom, bring the torch! Look! Look, the tunnel's wider here. It's a false wall. Round here to the side there's a narrow gap. Come on!"

"It's probably a trick, Lil. Grandpa Zhang wanted to put people off exploring any further."

We squeezed through the gap, only to be faced with a further setback. To our dismay, the only way ahead was up a steep climb of fallen rocks.

"Look, I think there used to be steps, Tom," I said, pointing to a couple of crumbled steps at the foot of the rock fall. "But that bit of wall has given way." At the top we could just see the small dark opening to another tunnel.

Each year after hay-making, Tom and I would climb up a huge mountain of stacked hay bales. We had developed a system – I went first and Tom was roped on to me. If he slipped, I'd pull him up. We'd seen people do it on films. Often though, once we were halfway up, we would let go on purpose and tumble down the bales into a hay-cushioned landing. We had nothing to rope ourselves together with now. I knew that a fall could mean death on the rocks at the foot of the chamber.

"We'll do it," said Tom reassuringly.

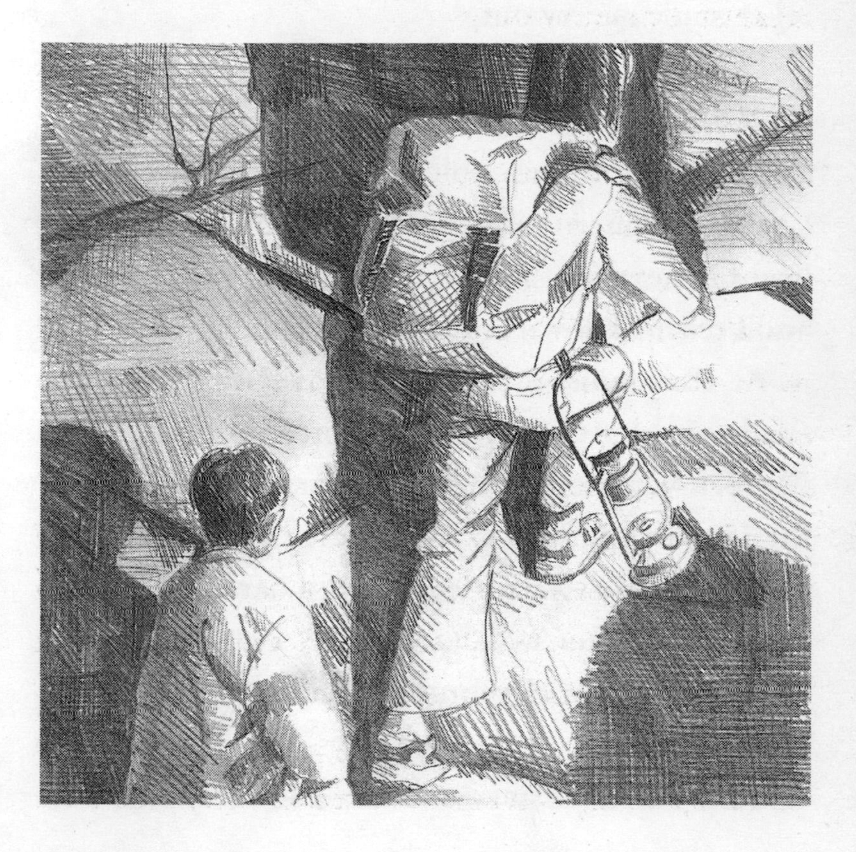

I felt as though my hands and feet were being torn to shreds as I clung to the jagged rocks. Slowly, we inched our way up. The lantern was swinging from the rucksack, making our shadows dance wildly as we climbed. Each foothold had to be tested before I put my weight on it. Slowly we climbed until we were tantalisingly close to the top.

My hands touched the uppermost rocks. The relief made me cry out.

"Tom, we made it!"

"Lil, hold on, I can't find my next step. I'm stuck!"

I managed to scramble up to the top of the fall. I held the lantern over the ledge so that Tom could find his next foothold. He stretched out his arm, and I reached down and took his hand in mine.

At that moment the rock gave way. Without thinking, I let go of the lantern to pull him on to the rock with both hands. We watched in horror as the lantern tumbled down the rocks to shatter at the bottom. We were plunged into darkness.

"We really can't go back now," I said, trembling as we sat on the ledge and I held on to Tom in the blackness.

Tom didn't answer me for a long time. "You

know the rucksack Lil, is it mine or yours?" he said at last.

"It's yours."

"Can you pass it to me?"

Carefully I pushed the rucksack on to his lap. He fumbled.

"They're in the pocket. I'm sure they are. Yes! Lil, it's all right. I found them. I've got the matches. I knew I'd packed them in Yangshuo."

"How many matches, Tom?" I said urgently now. "We need to know how many."

We were huddled together, staring hopelessly into the blackness. Tom opened the matchbox. My hands felt desperately awkward as I felt for one match at a time and put them in the palm of my hand.

"Eleven matches, Tom," I whispered. "They won't help us on the rock fall. Without a strong light, there's no way we'd get down alive. We'll have to go on. But we'll save the matches."

I longed to light one just here on the ledge for reassurance, but we knew that the opening to the tunnel was an arm's length away. We had to move as much as possible in the darkness.

I went first and Tom crawled behind me. Once

we were both in, I struck the first match. It spat and flickered. For a moment we saw that our tunnel was just an entrance to a huge cavern. I was shocked to see that there was a sheer drop ahead. Then I saw a ledge, like a path, at its side. We stayed on all fours. I dropped the match as it started to burn my fingers.

"You need to light another, Lil. We can't go along the path without it."

"OK," I said.

Our whispers echoed in the hollow depths around us. I don't know whether it was hunger or fear, but my stomach hurt now. My fingers slipped and the second match broke. The darkness was eerie.

"I'll do it Lil," said Tom.

I turned and he felt for my hands. He lit the second match. The path continued for a short way and then disappeared into the darkness.

"Go on Lil," said Tom.

We edged slowly forward, knowing only roughly how far we should go.

"Stop!" said Tom suddenly. "Lil stop! Let's light another match."

He did. The path disappeared behind a rock.

We made it to the rock before the match reached Tom's fingers and he dropped it into the cavern of dark below us. It disappeared like a firefly.

We sat beside the rock with the fourth match ready. I lit it and we both started in terror. Something white with huge nostrils stood before us.

"Tom!" I screamed. "Tom, it's OK! It's the camel! *It's the white jade camel...* the camel from the treasure box!"

I held the match higher, and before it died I saw bundles and boxes stacked together.

"The other treasures, they're all around us!" I said in wonder, "and the *tiger*! At the back, Tom. Did you see it?" I hugged him in the darkness. Tears of joy filled my eyes. "We've done it! We found it!"

Only then did the awful reality of our situation become clear to us. We had found Grandpa Zhang's treasure, but we might never get out of these tunnels alive. I'd never realised before that you could feel despair and elation at the same moment. We had exactly seven matches, two biscuits and half a flask of water left.

"Lily, let's light one more match, just to see the tiger again."

"Go on then," I said.

But when the match was lit, I didn't see the tiger. I was riveted to the flame. Tom's arm was outstretched. The flame danced. It swept to the left and flickered precariously.

"Lily, the tiger's eyes..."

"Tom, quick, look at the flame."

"Too late," cried out Tom as he dropped the match.

"Light another one, Tom, you must see."

Once again the flame swept to the left.

"Does it mean wind Lil, some sort of opening? There Lil, there... There's another tunnel to the right. Just above those rocks."

It was our only chance. We clambered over the rocks and into the tunnel.

The tunnel narrowed sharply moments after we stepped into it. We had to crawl again. Back in the suffocating darkness of the tunnel, I wondered if seeing the treasure had been just a dream. Suddenly I realised how tired and disorientated I felt. It seemed harder to move than before and my stomach still hurt.

"Lily, I think we're going upwards," said Tom. His voice was shaky and strange. We lit a match and found that the tunnel sloped steeply away. We were both breathing heavily now with the effort of moving so sharply uphill. I felt the same way as I used to at home when I went downstairs in the middle of the night to get a drink. Going back to bed in the dark, I'd start to run to escape imaginary ghouls that were stretching to grab my legs.

"Lily, I can see something."

Our eyes strained in the darkness. There *was* something. Gradually we were able to make out a very dim light. Neither of us spoke in case we broke the spell.

"Lily, it's daylight!" Tom called back to me. "Really it is. There's a rock in the way."

He grabbed my hand and pulled me up next to him. We pushed against the rock. It wouldn't budge.

"Come on Tom!"

Again we pushed with every last bit of strength we had – for Mum and Dad, for Primrose, for dreams come true, for breakfasts in our kitchen and the days of happiness to come. The rock gave way this time. It fell to one side. Glorious daylight and misty early morning sunshine came rushing to greet us as we crawled out into the fresh air. We looked at each other and we laughed, our faces were covered in smudges and dust. We realised we were on a grassy hillside overlooking the valley and just above our abandoned village where Aunt Li still slept unknowing. Our tiredness and aches vanished as excitement dawned.

"Race you to Aunt Li, Tom!" I shrieked as we tumbled down the hillside. Free of the tunnels at last.

Chapter Eighteen

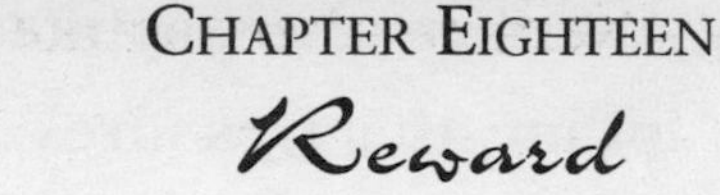

MANY THINGS HAPPENED after we ran down the hillside that morning. They are all jumbled in my mind whenever I think about them. Aunt Li had forgiven us for creeping out in the night. She said at least she never realised we'd gone until we woke her with our extraordinary story. Everyone at the hospital was so excited by our discovery that she was able to stay with us and to lead the officials back across Sleeping Tiger Mountain to the treasure.

After researching manuscripts back in Bcijing, archcologists found that our abandoned village had once been the site of a great palace. This was confirmed by the discovery of a small piece of rock with '平' on it, which means 'peace'. It would have been part of the name on one of the palace gates.

Grandpa Zhang and the wise old man had been very shrewd in hiding the treasures beneath it, because Chinese palaces were generally made of wood and did not have underground tunnels or dungeons. No one would have anticipated such labyrinths...

Important curators and Chinese officials had carried the treasures carefully out of the tunnels. They had laid them on our grassy hillside: the yellow dog, the white deer and that beautiful amber leaf with its butterfly that I'd become so familiar with. They lay there, no longer in miniature, but brilliant in the daylight.

It was only then that the truth had dawned on me. These were the treasures of the old Emperors of China. They belonged to the Chinese people. We couldn't keep the treasures for ourselves.

"There might be a reward," Tom had whispered hopefully as we had our photos taken beside the entrance to the tunnel.

We were thanked officially at an amazing dinner with many speeches, eight courses and more kinds of snake than I can ever forget. Aunt Li ate everything. Our reward was the honour we had gained in returning the treasures to the

Forbidden Palace. I had been silly to imagine anything else. Now we were powerless to save the farm.

After the dinner I was packing our bags. Grandma and Aunt Li came to me.

"Don't forget the treasure box, Lily Dragon," said Grandma Tsui.

"But, it belongs to the family... to you," I said.

"No Lily, it's yours now. You solved Grandpa Zhang's puzzle and fulfilled his dearest wishes. We are so proud of you. He would want you to have it. A keepsake to tell your children about."

I couldn't let Grandma see my tears. I turned away as if to wrap the treasure box in my jumpers. How could I tell Grandma that the treasure box would always be a symbol of our shattered dreams?

Aunt Li came to Chengdu Airport to see us off.

"Thank you for being so brilliant, Aunt Li," said Tom, giving her a hug.

Aunt Li sobbed as I hugged her goodbye. "Tell Bin Bin I love her children. Tell her I'll try to come to England soon."

Grandma and Aunt Li entreated us to stay longer, but Tom and I had to see Mum and Dad. And we wanted to say goodbye one last time to the home and animals we loved so much. The terrible truth was that the treasure had not saved the farm. It was to be sold in two days' time.

Chapter Nineteen

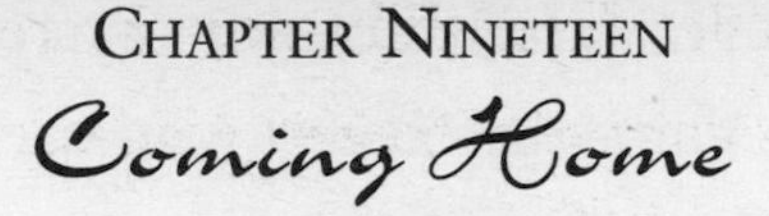

MUM STOOD LOST in thought at the Arrivals gate of the airport. She hadn't realised that we'd come through from the luggage hall until Tom screamed "Mum!" We both dropped our bags and rushed to fling our arms around her.

Her eyes looked tired, but she laughed as Tom took off his shoes there and then to show her the huge multicoloured bruise on his ankle.

"I banged it in the tunnel when I took the officials to see the treasure and I've got herbs to boil up and lay on it," he explained. "Aunt Li prepared them for me."

I held on to Mum's arm as we walked to the car. "I'm sorry. I meant it all to be different and I broke my promise to you because I told Tom everything."

She kissed my head just as she used to when

I was small. "Hush Lily Dragon. I'm proud of you, we both are. Thank goodness you are safe. I never thought that Grandpa Zhang's treasure might truly exist, let alone that you would find it. Your story was even in the newspapers over here – a huge photo of my two brave children and darling Li Li. You must tell Dad and me all about it."

"But the farm…" I began.

"The end of the month, two days... then we sign and leave." My mother spoke softly and firmly. She had been brave for so long now. "I must tell you though, Lily and Tom, try not to be too shocked. We have had to pack up a lot of things into boxes. We have each other and that's the main thing."

Tom, bursting with the tale of our adventure, sat in the front of the car and talked to Mum. I was in the back, lost in thought. I had resolved to be brave too, like Mum and Dad. Outside, the countryside looked bleaker and more wintry than I ever remembered at this time of year.

We turned into our lane past the clover field, the barn and the gap in the hedge. I suddenly realised, more than ever, how much I had missed it all. Next time we left, it would be for ever.

"The lambs!" I shouted. "Look Tom! Mum, can

you stop for a minute? We must see them."

Tom and I climbed over the stile to congratulate Primrose and to see the lambs who jostled foolishly with each other to get closer to their mother. They bleated and squealed as we patted and played with them.

Tom started back to the car. He wiped his eyes quickly when I caught up with him.

"What's going to happen, Lil? What can we do now?"

"Nothing my darlings," said my mother, who was standing at the stile. "Come on, you two. Into the car. There's nothing that *any* of us can do."

I remember watching a few intrepid leaves trembling in the winter wind above us and wondering if they had tried to resist the inevitability of the autumn. As we drew over the top of the hill we got our first glimpse of the farmhouse. My mother let out a sudden muffled cry.

"No, oh no!" She went quite pale and the car jolted to a stop.

"What's wrong, Mum?"

"They've come."

"Who?" I insisted.

"The lawyers... to sign the papers." A dark, shiny car was parked outside the farmhouse.

"But you said they weren't coming until the end of the month." I burst out. "We had two days... two days left to say goodbye." I fumbled with the car door and opened it. I climbed over the gate, ran across the fields and into the farmyard. I had to keep them away. I'd plead for nothing else but the time to say goodbye.

I rushed into the house – now stark and bare.

My dad, hearing my footsteps came in. "Lily, it's you!" he cried out and picked me up in a bear hug, kissing my cheek.

Then I saw her. A thin, smartly-dressed Chinese lady. She moved towards me, smiling warmly. I stared back at her, suddenly confused.

Tom burst into the kitchen. He faltered, seeing the lady.

"Lily," said my father as he hugged Tom. "This lady has come to see you both. Why don't you sit down."

At that moment it was my mother's turn to arrive and look surprised. My father beckoned her into the study.

"Lily and Tom," began the Chinese lady. "I am Ai Cheng. I am the Oriental Curator at the British Museum."

She held out a surprisingly wrinkled little hand. I shook it quickly. Tom squirmed in his seat. I knew he was going to ask a question.

"Why have you come to see us?" he said bluntly.

"Because I read about your story in the newspapers. I was transfixed by your search and I had to talk to you – for you talk of your Grandpa Zhang's treasure box, and I wondered if I could have a look at it?"

It was still in my bag on the kitchen floor. I got it out and unwrapped it from my jumpers. Ai Cheng gave a little intake of breath when she looked at it.

"Lily and Tom, do you realise what you have here? This is a great, great treasure; a work of art. The Empresses of China would collect boxes such as these. This is a particularly beautiful and historic example – all the more so since you have found the lost treasures it represents. This brings me to my proposal."

"Proposal?" I whispered in surprise.

"Yes. You see, Lily and Tom, I wonder if you would consider letting the Museum add your treasure box to its permanent collection? We would pay you, of course. I understand that it is an heirloom, but at least it would be in safe hands. Your family would have a free pass to the Museum whenever you wished, and your names would be on a plaque next to it as the benefactors of this precious..."

I could barely find my voice.

"Would it," I interrupted, "would it be enough to buy a whole farm?"

"Excuse me?" said Ai Cheng, looking puzzled.

"I mean, you say you would pay us..."

Ai Cheng smiled. "Lily, the sort of money the Museum is offering would buy you and Tom a whole farm each."

I felt very peculiar, like someone had taken away the feeling in my legs.

"I'm sorry," I gasped finally, "but I must tell Mum and Dad."

Grabbing Tom, I pulled him into the study, where Mum and Dad were sitting down amidst the packing cases.

"Mum and Dad," I said, holding both their hands in mine. "It's the treasure box. The Museum wants to keep it safe for us. They'll give us a lot of money. Primrose, the lambs, all your work, the farm, *everything* – it'll be saved for ever and ever."

"Yes, Lily," said my dad with his serious face. "But I don't think you should part with the treasure box unless you're sure you really want to."

"Of course I do," I said. "Ai Cheng will look after it. The farm is more important than *anything*."

I remember my dad sitting down and holding my mother's hand. I remember the tears in his eyes as we laughed at Tom, who was cheering so much that he fell off the edge of the sofa.

The Year of the Tiger was to be lucky after all.

Postscript

TONIGHT IS THE Festival of the Moon, the fifteenth day of the eighth moon. It's a chilly October evening, but we have hung our paper lanterns in the oak tree at the end of the clover field. Mine is the sun and Tom's is a tiger. We have sat for ages now on the lowest branch and watched the lights come on in the farmhouse.

"Let's celebrate it every year, Tom, for as long as we live. Right here by the oak tree, so we'll never forget."

"Forget what?" said Tom, munching his mooncake happily.

"Everything! The twins, Lucky Peanut, Sleeping Tiger Mountain, the Golden Water, lizards' tails, and what it felt like to know the farm was saved."

"I've been thinking," he said, nodding. "Isn't it

strange how Grandpa Zhang took all that trouble to hide the treasure, and the best treasure of all turned out to be his handmade box?"

I didn't answer him straightaway because I was trying to remember Grandma Tsui's words: "There are patterns in life that cannot be dismissed. To do so would affect our destiny."

Grandpa Zhang never knew, as he carved the treasure box three hundred years ago, that he was conceiving a pattern that would determine our destiny forever.

The Arctic Fox

Mary Ellis

Alex travels to the Arctic, with her explorer father, to return a little white fox to its natural habitat. At the Inuit school she meets Canny and discovers that *his* father has disappeared. The two children discover something that links Siku, the fox, with Canny's missing father and they set out on a journey that will change their lives forever.

'An evocative and moving story, and a convincing picture of Inuit culture.'
Mail on Sunday

Order Form

To order direct from the publishers, just make a list of the titles you want and fill in the form below:

Name ....

Address ....

....

....

Send to: Dept 6, HarperCollins Publishers Ltd, Westerhill Road, Bishopbriggs, Glasgow G64 2QT.

Please enclose a cheque or postal order to the value of the cover price, plus:

UK & BFPO: Add £1.00 for the first book, and 25p per copy for each additional book ordered.

Overseas and Eire: Add £2.95 service charge. Books will be sent by surface mail but quotes for airmail despatch will be given on request.

A 24-hour telephone ordering service is available to holders of Visa, MasterCard, Amex or Switch cards on 0141- 772 2281.

Collins
An *Imprint of* HarperCollins*Publishers*